Esca
The Country

Patsy Collins

For the enigmatic lensman -
Gary Davies

Chapter 1

With a sigh of relief, Leah indicated to exit the motorway. It seemed she really was going to escape from the city. She couldn't run away from herself, but there were plenty of things she could leave behind, such as the office at Prophet Margin where she'd worked until she'd been suspended yesterday morning. She was also leaving Adam behind.

She blinked several times to clear the moisture that formed in her eyes as she thought of Adam. If she could just get him to come down to Kent, away from the stress and strains of his job, maybe he'd be able to concentrate on his feelings and they'd recapture some of the love and passion they'd once shared. Until then, a short separation might do them both good. Adam would miss her after a day or two, wouldn't he? Leah wasn't yet ready to give up on the relationship and her hopes for their future.

It was no good her worrying; much better to think of something positive. It will be great to see her aunt again. Leah hadn't really spoken to Jayne for ages. Not since... well not since she'd met Adam, come to think of it. She hadn't visited Jayne's smallholding for an even longer period. Back then, it had been Jayne's parents - Leah's Granny and Granddad who'd run the place and Leah had been a visiting schoolgirl. She sighed again as she remembered how carefree and

1

happy she'd been then.

A chat with Jayne would soon cheer her up and then Leah could relax in scented bath water before giggling the evening away over a glass of home-made wine. Her worries stood no chance against competition like that.

Leah wondered why she hadn't come down to Winkleigh Marsh before. Jayne frequently invited her but Adam had never found a free weekend.

"Come on your own then, Leah. I can always fix you up with a dishy tractor driver or the lad who mucks out the pigs," Jayne had urged.

"You've got staff now?" Surely the tiny farm couldn't need a full time tractor driver.

Jayne laughed. "Of course not. I do have neighbours though. Lots of strong, fit male neighbours."

"Tempting, but no. Hopefully we'll be able to come next month," Leah had replied, but somehow they'd always had other more pressing invitations; golf matches with Adam's acquaintances or dinner parties with people he hoped to impress.

Yesterday evening though, when he'd seen how upset she was by her suspension from work, Adam had suggested a break might do her good. Leah immediately thought of visiting her aunt at Primrose Cottage. Leah had rung Jayne to say she unexpectedly had some free time.

Jayne must have realised, from Leah's subdued tone, something was wrong but she hadn't asked any difficult questions, instead urging Leah to come as soon as she liked.

"If you came now, the roads would be quiet."

"I can't just drive down now."

"Oh, all right then. I'll see you for lunch tomorrow."

Leah had almost laughed with relief. Just like that, she'd been offered the chance to escape. There would be problems in the countryside too, but they wouldn't be caused by irregularities in complicated financial dealings or a man scared of commitment and, as she was a visitor, they wouldn't affect Leah.

Leah was glad of the sat nav Adam had fitted in her car. Although she'd spent much of her childhood at Winkleigh Marsh, she hadn't visited since. The device directed her down yet another narrow lane, warning her of the sharp bend ahead, but not the tractor which made it impossible for Leah to get around that bend anytime soon. She didn't mind driving slowly. It was pleasant to look at the scenery as she drove along. Even in the depths of winter, and despite a few lumps of mud on the road, the country lane was attractive. She spotted a deep green holly bush and ivy growing into the crowns of trees which had shed their leaves. They weren't oaks or silver birches, the only trees Leah could confidently identify. She recognised several landmarks on the way to Aunt Jayne's smallholding. The watermill, a milestone and even an old signpost looked exactly as she remembered. She'd been away to long, but not so long she felt a stranger.

The tractor pulled over into a field entrance, allowing Leah to pass. She drove slowly, partly to avoid scratching her car's shiny pink paintwork and partly to get a good look at the driver and tease her aunt about her idea of good looking men.

Leah looked straight into the cab at the driver's smiling face, registering an abundance of curly brown hair and broad shoulders. Very nice! She'd thought Jayne had been kidding about the presence of a dishy tractor driver, but apparently not. There'd be no teasing now, just admiration of her aunt's excellent taste.

Leah waved to the driver in thanks for his consideration in allowing her to overtake. He returned her acknowledgement. Leah was sorry that concentrating on the road ahead meant she couldn't fully appreciate his cheeky grin.

Jayne must have heard or seen Leah's car because she was waiting in the yard, dog at her side, to yank open the door and hug Leah the moment she stopped.

"It's so good to see you, lovey. My but you've got thin. Don't they have any food up there in London then?"

Leah hugged Jayne in return and kissed her cheek. "It's good to see you, too." She bent to stroke the dog whose front end was trying desperately to stay still under the immense pressure of the waggy tail. "You must be Tarragon."

As Leah made a fuss of the English Setter, she studied her aunt. Jayne's rich red hair was cut short for practicality, but the choppy style suited her and showed off her lively, heart shaped face. Leah wasn't sure if she was wearing mascara, but if so it was her only trace of make up. Jayne's clothes weren't at all fashionable, but the bright colours were cheerful and drew attention to her neat curves. There were no bags or dark circles under her eyes and the faint lines on her face were definitely laughter lines not wrinkles.

Leah had much longer hair in the same vibrant shade, was fifteen years younger, fashionably dressed and immaculately made up, but she didn't put Jayne in the shade. Leah felt they could easily have passed for sisters.

"How long's it been?" Jayne asked.

"Too long," Leah admitted. They'd met in London and at various family functions, but not often.

"It has. And for your parents. I know they're loving life in New Zealand, but I miss my big brother. Letters and e-mails are great, but no substitute for a hug."

"They say the same. I know they want to come and see you."

Jayne helped Leah carry in her bags and showed

her to her room. Tarragon came into the house, but didn't accompany them upstairs. Unlike the bedroom Leah shared with Adam, in this room there was no TV, no phone socket, no computer. Just a big comfy bed, wardrobe and bedside table.

"You sort yourself out, lovey and I'll put the kettle on."

Leah didn't bother to unpack. She just shoved her cases into the bottom of the wardrobe and took her wash bag into the bathroom. Once she'd freshened up, she sat on the bed and put her alarm clock on the bedside table next to the vase of evergreens and snowdrops Jayne had picked to welcome her. Force of habit had made her pack the clock, but Leah doubted she'd be setting the alarm during her stay.

On the wall was a photograph of May, Leah's grandmother and Jayne's mother. Although Leah had seen the picture before, she was still startled by May's beauty. It wasn't just the woman's name that had seen her crowned May Queen several times in her youth. Granddad had always assured Leah, and probably Jayne too, that she was just as pretty, but he'd have said the same whatever she'd looked like. It was still hard to believe she'd never see them again except in photographs.

Leah wandered over to the window and looked out. The lovely view over farmland and woods Leah remembered from her childhood was still much the same. Leah sent Adam a text, to let him know she'd arrived safely, before going back downstairs.

Jayne had made a pot of tea and set the table for lunch. She served a big slice of home-baked steak pie. Leah accepted the offered plate and helped herself to vegetables. It wasn't true that Leah had lost weight, in fact for the last few weeks she'd been comfort eating. She sighed.

"Something wrong?" Jayne asked.

"No, this looks and smells delicious." Leah knew Jayne hadn't really been asking about the food, but wasn't ready to admit her problem was more than a silly misunderstanding at work. That she'd known for a while things weren't right. Leah took a bite of crisp pastry and succulent meat. It was delicious.

"I'm glad this is home-made," she said as Jayne encouraged her to have a second helping. "There's no panel on the pack to tell me how much saturated fat and how many calories per 100g."

"There's no need to worry about that anyway as you're here for a change, not a rest, my girl. I intend making you work for your supper, lovey."

Great; physical work might help Leah get things into perspective. With any luck she'd be working hard enough to burn off all the food she'd eat. Not that it mattered for a few days; Jayne wouldn't make any sarcastic comments even if her clothes were a little more filled out than the designer would have liked.

"Do you want to talk, or just chat?" Jayne asked.

"Chat, for now," Leah replied. If possible she was going to forget her problems just long enough for her to gather the strength to tackle them.

"Suits me - there's plenty of gossip to catch up on. G-B has made some changes and you remember my friend Chantelle? Well, you're never going to believe what she's been getting up to and..."

As Leah listened to an outline of the forthcoming gossip-fest she studied her aunt.

"You look great, Jayne."

"Nothing like as good as you're going to look once you've got a decent night's sleep, some fresh air and tried a few of my lotions and potions."

"You've got a herbal remedy to cure accusations of fraud?"

"Fraud! Leah who could say such a thing about you? You've always been completely honest, even as a little kid. I remember times when a little white lie would have got you out of trouble but you wouldn't say it. Remember when you tripped and broke a whole basket of eggs?"

Leah started to shake her head, but stopped as the memory of smashed shells burst yolks and a feeling of guilt came back to her. "Yes. I'd seen Granddad carrying a bucket down to the lambs and I thought I'd miss feeding them. I ran after him instead of taking the eggs in as I'd been told."

"Yes and you admitted as much and gave Mum your pocket money to try to make up for it. There's no way you'd commit fraud, Leah."

"Oh, Jayne, I'm so glad I came." She wanted to cry at the relief of being believed.

"It'll be all right, lovey. I know I don't yet know exactly what's wrong or how it can be put right, but I'm sure we'll think of something."

"Everything is wrong, that's what."

Tears trickled down Leah's cheeks as Jayne pulled her into a hug.

Why, when she'd stumbled into Adam's office, after her boss had told her about the irregularities in her biggest account, hadn't Adam done that? His 'let's wait and see and look into all the facts before doing anything' approach might be realistic and no doubt he was working behind the scenes at Prophet Margin right now in ways of which she was unaware, but when she'd told him, all she'd wanted him to do was hug her and say everything was going to be OK.

After a few minutes of crying, Leah felt calmer. She blew her nose. "Sorry, Aunt Jayne."

"Leah, you can't keep calling me Aunt. It was OK when you were a kid, but now it makes me feel grey haired and wrinkly, like Miss Marple."

"Like who?"

"The fluffy old lady who solved half the crimes in the Agatha Christie books."

"Thought that was Hercule Poirot."

"He solved the other half."

Leah had a feeling Jayne might be able to help with half of her problems too. Of course she could, wasn't that why Leah had rushed down here?

"So, we do a few chores this afternoon, then after supper we can have a glass or two of cowslip wine and you can tell me all about it, how's that sound?" Jayne asked.

"Like an excellent plan."

"You wash up then and I'll go and find you some clothes for you to work in. I don't suppose you've got anything suitable?"

"Not unless you want me to take dictation or update a few spreadsheets?"

"I could do with some help on the computer, but that's not what I've got in mind for you."

Leah knew her clothes were unsuitable, but they were all she had. Adam's idea of getting close to nature was to watch a documentary or hang bird feeders on their balcony, so she didn't have any use for practical outdoor wear. Jayne lent her some scruffy jeans, a thick sweater and a warm coat, all of which fitted very well and were surprisingly comfortable and a pair of wellingtons which didn't and weren't.

"I think you're going to need extra socks to hold those on your feet," Jayne said.

Jayne's idea of a few chores started with repairs to a fence around the chicken run. Leah broke two finger nails in as many minutes and went inside to file the others down. It wasn't just in terms of clothing that she was unprepared for a stay on a farm.

The next little job was to chop and stack firewood. After that, they fed the pigs. Tarragon lolloped along with them, managing to stay mud free as he criss-crossed the small yard and dodged in and out of animal pens. Leah stopped occasionally to stroke his grey silky head and check her phone. There was no message from Adam. Each time Jayne saw Leah snap shut the phone and thrust it into her pocket, she dragged her off to a new task.

"I'm getting on much quicker with you to help me; I think we'll have time to sort out the sheep before we deal with Rosemary."

First they had to catch the six sheep which was a job in itself, then Leah had to stand with a leg each side of the squirming animal and wrap her arms around its neck so Jayne could trim its feet. Once each was released it bounded away, evidently delighted with its pedicure. Leah didn't have the energy to bound away after the job was done. She was convinced she'd be needing the cowslip wine intravenously.

"What sort of animal is Rosemary?" she gasped once the last woolly wrestling partner had joined his tag team.

"A beautiful Jersey cow. You're going to love her."

"I'm sorry, Jayne, but there's no way I can hold a cow down."

Jayne shrieked with laughter which Leah hoped was a sign she was mistaken in her belief she'd have to manhandle the creature.

"Come on, you townie," Jayne said. "Don't worry, we're just going to milk her."

Rosemary was indeed beautiful. She had the most amazing chocolate eyes with long lashes which made Leah remember the tractor driver she'd seen earlier. True she'd not been close enough to see his lashes, but she had enough imagination to picture them. Unlike the dishy tractor driver, Rosemary also had a soft velvety nose which snuffled at the hand Leah was coaxed into holding out. The cow was dainty and incredibly calm. She stood still whilst Jayne sat on the floor of her stable and milked her into a large bucket. Rosemary looked as though she was chewing an especially good toffee.

"Chewing the cud," Jayne explained. "They have to do that to properly digest their food. You know a cow or sheep is relaxed if they chew."

Leah should probably be chewing as she was relaxed enough to pass out.

Once Jayne had enough milk in her bucket, she let two young calves into Rosemary's pen.

"Twins?" Leah guessed.

"No. These are a couple of Angus bulls, I've bought in."

"So neither are hers?" The cow was licking them as though she was fond of them.

"No. She had a heifer. I don't need another cow to keep as I already have Rosepetal, Rosemary's calf from a couple of years ago and a jersey heifer's not much good for meat, so I sold it and bought these two."

"So these will become roast beef?" It seemed sad, but Jayne had to make a living somehow.

"Not just any roast beef; the finest locally reared, organic roast beef. I sell all my animals and eggs direct to a local butcher now. He knows for sure where the meat comes from and that it's great quality and I actually get a decent price."

Leah nodded, but really she was too tired to take in details of Jayne's business plan. Her muscles ached, joints felt hot and hands stung as Leah hauled herself up off the barn floor.

A soak in bathwater containing a liberal quantity of Jayne's home-made herbal bath oil revived her considerably. Her back and biceps stopped throbbing and the painful blisters on each palm subsided to a warm tingling.

"It's a special mix to soothe aching muscles," Jayne explained as she handed Leah the bottle. "I got the recipe from the book you sent me for my birthday."

Leah remembered the book. She'd been unable to think of a suitable birthday gift and had asked Adam for inspiration.

"What does she like?" he'd asked.

Leah had reeled off a list of things she knew Jayne enjoyed or was interested in. Adam's suggestion had been a garden centre voucher which hadn't seemed a bad idea. A couple of days later though he'd returned from one of his regular trips around the local second-hand bookshops with an exquisite book on herbal remedies. It was antique and beautifully illustrated with hand coloured plates.

He hadn't let her repay him, saying he was embarrassed to admit how much he'd spent on a lot of old mumbo jumbo. "From what you told me, it does seem perfect for her though."

It did. The cover was of powder blue leather; Jayne's favourite colour. The author's surname was Jayne and inside the book was a bookmark decorated with pressed primroses. Jayne had still been squealing with delight when she'd called to thank Leah. Even better, the recipe actually seemed to work and the burning ache in Leah's thighs and biceps melted away to a dull throb.

The chicken stew and dumplings followed by baked apple and thick Jersey cream further helped Leah's recovery.

Life in the countryside was pretty much living up to her expectations. She had a comfortable room, the comfort of her aunt Jayne, good food and no more tasks for the day. Already she was almost as relaxed as Tarragon who pretended to snooze in his bed, but occasionally opened one big brown eye to check for dropped crumbs. Leah had enough sense to know this break wouldn't be the same as the idyllic summer holidays she'd spent with Jayne, her grandparents and sometimes her own parents. Life on a smallholding in winter would be cold, muddy and hard work. Still there was a toasty fire in front of her and the promise of cowslip wine for now and the hope of working things out with Adam. It could be a lot worse.

Leah checked her phone and was pleased to see she'd received a text.

'Heard wot happened. Dont believe it. Call if want 2 chat.'

She stared at it for several moments until realising it was from her colleague Rachel, not her boyfriend. Why would Rachel call? Leah couldn't imagine wanting to chat to her about the problems she was facing. Still it was good to know not everyone assumed she was guilty. Leah made another attempt to contact Adam, but had to be content with leaving a message on his voicemail.

It was reassuring to know Adam had been mistaken and not everyone at work was shunning her. Maybe, after she'd enjoyed a few days with

Jayne, all her problems would be resolved. The only potential fly in the ointment was the G-B Jayne had alluded to. Oliver Gilmore-Bunce was a client of Prophet Margin, the stockbrokers and investors she worked for, and a right pain even before he'd become the source of her current problem. The less Leah had to do with Oliver Gilmore-Bunce, the happier she'd be.

Jayne poured golden liquid into two tiny glasses. "They're liqueur glasses really, so we'll need a lot of refills, but they're so pretty, I just have to use them for cowslip wine."

"Is the wine really made from cowslips? I know there are always masses around the cottage, but I can't imagine you picking buckets of them."

"It really is made from cowslips... and a few other things. Actually, I buy a simple winemaking kit and just add a few cowslip flowers. Still tastes pretty good though, I think?"

Leah accepted her drink and took a sip. "Wonderful." She inspected the glass. It was beautifully decorated with a posy of cowslips.

"What lovely engraving! Where did you get them?"

"It's an etching actually, and I got them from a rather nice man who made them for me as a gift for services rendered."

"Aunt Jayne!"

"It's a very good story actually, but as you've called me Aunt again, you've made me feel too old to tell it you."

"Sorry," Leah said. She wasn't particularly sorry. If it really was a good story, Jayne wouldn't be able to resist telling her.

"So, what's the matter then?" Jayne asked after refilling their glasses.

Leah took a deep breath. Where should she start? "I've been suspended from work. There are discrepancies in a customer's account which they need to investigate and the computer records seem to show I've been defrauding him of tens of thousands of pounds."

"But you haven't?" She asked it as a question, but Leah knew she wasn't being accused.

"No."

"So they'll find out that it's all a mistake. I'm no computer or finance expert, but I'm sure that if you've not done something nobody'll be able to prove you did."

"No, I suppose not."

"Are you in a union or anything?"

"I do belong to a professional organisation and I've let them know. They'll ensure the situation is properly investigated and I'm not dismissed without cause. Prophet Margin have to keep me on full pay, so it's in their interests to get this resolved as soon as possible." Put like that, it didn't seem as though she was in too much trouble. True, embezzlement was a serious crime that could lead to imprisonment. It was equally true that she was innocent.

"And what's that Adam doing about it? He's a computer expert, supposedly. Didn't he go and tell them he knows you'd never do such a thing and show them where they'd gone wrong?"

Jayne was getting close to the real problem.

"No. I thought he might. He can't really though. He's in charge of I.T. but the investment side is separate and he can't get involved. He said it was better to be patient and that if they knew about us they'd just think he was biased or might believe he was involved or..."

"He didn't stick up for you at all?"

"Well, it's complicated."

"I bet. And what's that about knowing about you? Has he kept it secret that you're living together?"

"Not secret, just..."

"Complicated?"

It sounded weak, even to Leah.

"Your whole life seems complicated since you've met him."

"I know." Leah took another sip of her drink. It was only recently she'd admitted, even to herself, that her relationship with Adam wasn't making her happy. She still wasn't sure what she wanted to do about that. "He wanted to keep his personal and professional lives separate."

"What? He's a computer geek, not a pop star."

Leah didn't reply as she'd often had the same thought. His insistence on keeping his distance at work might seem perfectly natural to him, but it hurt her. It felt as though he was almost ashamed of her.

"You expect him to stick up for your reputation when he's not honest with them?" Jayne continued.

"It wasn't like that," she mumbled. She wasn't even convincing herself. She longed to confess her worries to Jayne, but that meant facing up to the truth and she wasn't quite ready for that.

Adam said their relationship wasn't anyone's business but theirs. Business was the right word to use. Adam bought their flat as an investment; Leah wanted it to be a home. Adam wanted a pre-nup agreement before he'd commit to marriage. While Leah could see it was sensible, she didn't want to be planning the divorce before they'd even picked a date for the wedding.

Jayne said, "His weird behaviour is none of my business either. Your happiness is, so let's see what we can do to cheer you up."

"A refill might help," Leah suggested, holding out her glass.

Jayne took the hint. As that didn't seem enough to distract Jayne from probing deeper into Leah's problems, she got up and stroked Tarragon. She remembered that as a child, the only animals she'd heard Jayne say a bad word about were dogs. Even then she put the blame on irresponsible owners, rather than creatures who were just doing what came naturally.

"I was surprised when you told me you'd got a dog," Leah said, "But now I've met him it makes much more sense. He really is adorable."

"Useful too. I don't get other people's dogs wandering all over the place now. The owners see he's about and put theirs on leads. Tarragon actually helps round up the sheep. You saw that today."

"He was helpful, yes."

"Everyone needs a little help," Jayne said.

"That's why I've come to you. Is there any more helpful stuff left in that bottle?"

As Leah got ready for bed, she thought over what Jayne had said. Jayne trusted that as Leah was innocent then her problems would soon be solved. Leah was less sure. She might get her job back, but her hopes of a happy marriage and, eventually, children had never seemed further away. Leah wasn't going to let unhappy thoughts spoil her visit before it had begun, so tried to picture something pleasant as she went to sleep. For some reason, the image that came to mind was that of a tractor on a country lane and a curly haired driver waving to her.

Chapter 2

Leah awoke to hear a cock crow and assorted animals calling either to each other, or for food. She groaned. She'd forgotten the peace of the countryside, whilst real enough in the evenings, was a complete myth at dawn. Still, she had slept right through the night which was something of a novelty in recent months. She reached out an arm for her phone. No messages and no missed calls. Of course not, it was too early. Leah turned over and went back to sleep.

When she woke for the second time, the world outside her window was again peaceful. Presumably Jayne was already up and had fed those animals which had been making a fuss. Perhaps she'd better get up too, lying awake thinking was something to avoid.

She groaned again as she got out of bed. Jayne's herbal bath oil had done a good job the previous evening, but it hadn't been able to entirely prevent Leah's muscles stiffening overnight. After a few stretches, she felt a little better. Her aches and pains were the result of unaccustomed work, not any actual injury. Although her hands looked as though they'd

Patsy Collins

never even heard of a manicure, the blisters were now no more than faint red marks.

As she came out the bathroom, Leah heard Jayne moving about downstairs. She checked her bedside clock so she'd know what time Jayne was normally up and could avoid disturbing her normal routine. It was just after ten-thirty. Lea quickly dressed and went downstairs.

Jayne asked, "How do you like your eggs these days?"

"To be honest, it's so long since I've had a fried egg, I'm not really sure."

Jayne cracked eggs into the pan, sizzled them lightly, then added one to each plate already brimming with bacon, mushrooms, chipolatas, tomatoes and large slices of something golden brown.

"I thought I'd missed breakfast," Leah said as she squirted HP sauce onto her plate.

"I don't like it too early, so I feed the animals and milk Rosemary first. I can relax and enjoy it that way."

"So it really is half ten?" Leah asked as she cut open one of the crispy brown slices. She took an experimental nibble.

"Yes. I guess you slept well?"

Leah's mouth was now full of potato, fried until crisp in fresh butter so instead of speaking, she

22

nodded in agreement.

"Not been doing that much lately?"

"No, but... "

"It's all right, lovey, you needn't talk about it if you don't want to."

"It's Adam. Things haven't been going too well." She shrugged. "I suppose everyone goes through bad patches?"

"Of course they do. Now enjoy your breakfast."

The ache in her muscles convinced Leah she'd worked off everything she'd eaten yesterday, so she blocked out all thought of calorie counts and ate.

"I'll wash up, you go and give Adam a call. Maybe he'll have some news by now."

"I keep trying, he doesn't answer."

"Use my house phone."

Leah obediently went into the hall and dialled Adam's number on Jayne's old fashioned cream and green phone. She thought if Adam was too busy to pick up when he saw her number flash up he was hardly likely to answer one he didn't recognise. She was wrong.

"Oh, Leah, hi. Sorry I didn't reply to your message yesterday, but things were crazy here and then the phone was flat. I don't think it's holding a charge properly."

"Ah."

The phone on his desk was evidently working, but maybe there was a good reason for him not having tried to contact her.

"So, everything all right with your aunt?" Adam asked.

"Yes. She's feeding me up and I've been helping with the sheep and mending fences."

"Good, good. Sounds like she needs your help. Perhaps you should stay there for a while?"

The idea was appealing. Her body had been worked hard, but her mind and emotions had been granted some much needed rest.

"Yes. I feel less tense already. I did need a break, you were right. Maybe you could join us for the weekend?"

"Leah, we've split up, remember?"

"Adam, no! That's what I said, in the heat of the moment, but not what I meant. You must know that."

He hadn't liked it when she'd said that if he wasn't prepared to offer some kind of commitment and emotional support, she'd be better off without him. Perhaps that was because it was the first time she'd really stuck up for herself.

"It would appear that I no longer know what you want, or perhaps never had the ability to provide it."

"You do. I just wanted you to acknowledge our relationship rather than acting as though you're ashamed of me and I didn't think a pre-nup was exactly romantic and..." she broke off her explanation when she realised he was talking over her.

"Of course, if you decide to come back to London in the near future you can stay in the flat. We can make some arrangement."

"Arrangement? It's my home and of course I'll be back. I can hardly commute to work from Winkleigh Marsh."

"Maybe you'll get a job nearer there."

"I have a job! It was all just a misunderstanding. They'll realise that soon enough."

"Maybe if you were to pay in the missing money?"

"No way. That'd look as though I was guilty and anyway, you know I don't have that amount of cash."

He didn't reply.

"You actually think I could have done it, don't you?"

She could hear sounds from his office in the background, but he still didn't answer her.

"Adam?"

There was a click and the line went dead.

She replaced the handset with such force, the hall table shook and a pot of pens fell off.

Leah returned to the kitchen where she saw Tarragon hanging his head and Jayne vigorously drying plates.

"You heard?" Leah asked.

Jayne nodded. "Some of it, yes."

"We rowed when he got back from work the day I was suspended. He twisted round my words until I said I didn't think we had a future together. I thought by now he'd realise it was just because I was upset and angry, but he won't even discuss it."

"The rat! I never liked him."

"You've never even met him." Leah didn't have enough fight left to put much indignation into her voice.

"No, but I don't like that he never came here. It makes me feel like he's got something to hide. What sort of live-in boyfriend isn't interested in meeting the family?"

Leah had no answer to that as it was a question she'd been pushing to the back of her mind for quite a while.

"Oh, lovey. I'm sorry," Jayne said. "Don't take any notice of a grumpy old spinster like me. What do I know? Things have a way of sorting themselves out. You're too upset to think straight now. We'll have a talk later and see what's to be done."

"Thanks, Jayne." Leah blew her nose.

"Come on now. Fresh air will do you good. We'll let the chickens into their new run and see how they like it."

"Yes, OK. Will I need the wellies?"

"No, we'll stay in the yard this morning."

Leah changed into her trainers.; she'd probably be working harder than she ever did in the gym. She'd only packed them because she didn't want Adam to get the idea she'd be letting herself go while she was away. His shocked face when she'd mentioned looking forward to the roast dinners and desserts with lashings of creamy custard Jayne would serve made her feel guilty even before she'd left, let alone taken the first delicious bite.

"You'd better use some of this too, on those soft townie hands of yours." She gave Leah a small pot of cream. "Put it on before you go outside or get your hands wet. I use it all the time and hadn't realised how well it works until I saw your hands."

Leah rubbed the greasy lotion into her chapped skin. It did feel as though it would be an effective barrier to the cold, dirt and wet.

The chickens seemed rather shy to start with, despite Tarragon doing his best to gently nudge them outside.

"Sit," Jayne commanded. "Give them time to get used to the idea, you impatient hound, you."

Once the bravest couple of hens stuck their beaks out into the sunshine, the rest followed. Soon they were all pecking at the fresh grass and scratching in the dirt, abandoning the eggs for Jayne and Leah to collect.

"This is easier than I remember," Leah said as she filled her basket with warm eggs. "I used to have to fumble around under the hens and some of them pecked."

"That's because your parents usually left you with us at Easter. By then the chickens are going broody and want to sit on the eggs and hatch them."

"Ah. I always thought you made me get the eggs from the meanest ones, just to hear me squeal when they went for me."

"Might of done." Jayne gave a naughty grin.

"What? Ooooh you, you... You can wrestle your own sheep in future."

"Talking of which, I've got a good job for you now."

"Sheep?"

"No, not quite."

"Not quite in what way? Crikey, it's not Llamas is it? Those things scare me."

Jayne snorted with mischievous laughter. "I'd almost forgotten about that!"

"Was that another of your plans to make me squeal?"

"Well..."

"You really were a meany. I was only seven!" Leah did her best schoolgirl petulant pout.

"Yeah, it was a bit mean. Funny though and I swear I didn't know they were quite so defensive of their kids. I didn't know your little legs could go that fast either."

"Good thing for you they could. You'd have had a lot of explaining to Granny May if I'd got squished." She folded her arms and tried to look aggrieved, but soon smiled at Jayne's amusement.

"One day, I'll get my own back."

"I seem to remember you did at the time. Those frogs didn't do a lot for my love life."

This time Leah giggled and Jayne tried to look miffed.

"So, what's this lovely job, then?" Leah asked.

"I thought we'd make a start preparing for the orphan lambs."

"That's really sad."

"The lambs?"

"Yes. They're lovely, but it's sad so many are still orphaned."

Jayne laughed. "I'd forgotten what a townie you are! They're not really orphaned, you chump. They're taken from mothers, who have three or four lambs, to give the others a better chance."

"Oh!" She did feel a bit daft for never having learned that, especially as the thought of their dead mothers had so upset her as a child.

They swept the pens, clearing cobwebs and dust. Then sterilised the bottles and buckets that would be used to feed the lambs.

"I used to love feeding the lambs when I came down here as a kid," Leah said. "They're so cute the way their little bodies waggle when they suck at the bottles and how they skip about and jump off the bales and things."

Jayne giggled. "You were obsessed! I remember if we couldn't find you we went straight to the lamb pen. You used to curl up in a ball and let the lambs jump on you."

"Ah, you remember that? I wish I was staying long enough to do it again. Not the climbing frame bit perhaps, but feeding them."

"You'd be more than welcome, lovey, but they're not coming for a few weeks. The trouble with your job will be sorted by then, won't it?"

"Yes," Leah said. If it was going to be sorted at all, it shouldn't take long. Her other problems would take longer, but hiding away in the country wouldn't solve them.

"You can come down anyway though, for the weekend or something. There won't be any... Oh."

"Won't be anything to stop me? I don't know."

"Oh don't worry yourself. You've had a shock over this money stuff, that's why you and Adam have rowed. It'll sort itself out soon enough if that's what you want."

Jayne was right, Leah had suffered a shock. Right now, she wasn't entirely sure what she did want.

"Right, let's see about some lunch," Jayne said.

Leah didn't think she could possibly be hungry after her cooked breakfast, but the smell of leek and potato soup proved her wrong. The soup was followed by the rice pudding Jayne had put into the Aga after breakfast.

"What would you like to do this afternoon? Anything in particular?" Jayne asked, as they washed up.

"I hadn't really thought..."

"Well, you know I'm always busy. You're welcome to tag along with me as much as you like and I'll have plenty you can help with, but feel free to go off and do your own thing whenever you like."

"Great, thanks. What's your next job?" Leah asked as she wiped the rice pudding dish.

"Cleaning out the pigs."

"Thought you had a dishy young man to help with that?"

"No sorry. I made him up." Jayne pulled off her rubber gloves and draped them over the tap.

"I rather thought you had. Maybe I'll give the pigs a miss today. I'm not quite ready for them yet. I'll just have a walk round, see what I remember."

"Would you like Tarragon for company?"

The dog seemed to know he was under discussion and turned his head to look at Leah. She was sure he was doing his best to give a winning smile.

"Will he be OK with me?"

"Yes, he's taken to you. In any case, he's good on the lead and if he knows you've got a pocket full of treats he'll never be too far away."

"I won't be long."

"Take as long as you like. I expect you could do with a chance to think and hopefully the walk will bring back some happy memories too."

No making her feel guilty? No of course not; Jayne wasn't like that. She wouldn't be sulking when Leah came back either. To be fair to Adam he probably made his plans for evenings out and weekends away with the hope of pleasing her and often she'd been delighted with the interesting places he'd taken her. He never reacted well if she didn't immediately go along with all his suggestions though. It was a pleasant change to be able to say and do what she liked without fearing a frosty reaction.

Leah decided to walk over neighbouring farmland to the nearest shop. Her decision had almost nothing to do with the fact that her chosen route gave her the best possible chance of bumping into a tractor driver. As a child, she'd loved the freedom of being allowed to make that walk alone to spend her pocket money, whenever her visits coincided with Jayne being away at university. It was just over a mile each way by footpath, more than a six mile round trip by car. Shame the shops hadn't been that far away when she'd quit smoking. Despite ready access to cigarettes then she'd found the willpower to stop; she'd find the strength to get through her current difficulties and make a fresh start.

Although Tarragon didn't pull, holding his lead was making her tired arms ache. Even switching from hand to hand didn't help much. Once on open grassland, Leah unclipped his lead. He bounded off, his grey speckled ears flapping up and down with each long stride. He repeatedly came rushing back to her side before setting off somewhere else. She laughed at his eagerness to go about the important doggy business of sniffing and exploring combined with his desire to bound back towards her, wanting only an affectionate greeting and rub of his silky head. Such a change from big business and people only interested in money.

She shook her head to dislodge her negative thoughts. Her fresh start would include Adam. Could it take place in the countryside? They'd be free of the vicious circle of needing more and more money to pay for things that didn't make her happy. Clothes for work functions she didn't want to attend, Blackberries and notebooks to stay in touch with people she didn't like.

Leah couldn't see Tarragon. She yelled his name. Moments later, he was careening down the bank towards her. He managed to slow up just enough that he didn't quite knock her down as he skidded up against her borrowed wellington boots.

"Good boy!" She gave him a meaty chew as a reward for returning so promptly.

Leah reached into her pocket to check her phone. There was no point; if it had rung she'd have heard it. Anyway it wasn't like Adam to apologise, even when he knew he was in the wrong and this time it seemed he wanted to put all the blame on her.

She looked up to see Tarragon hauling himself over a wooden style and lollop off at speed towards a herd of cows. They were black and white; great rangy things, not cute Jerseys like Jayne's house cows Rosemary and her daughter Rosepetal. Leah, worried the dog might chase them or get chased himself, called to him. He seemed not to hear.

Leah clambered over the style and followed, shouting the dog's name. He stopped, turned and bounded back to her. When he reached her side, he trotted along quietly, occasionally sniffing her pocket. Eventually she took the hint and remembered the treats.

"OK, boy, you can have one."

He unrolled his tongue and used it to gently take the snack from her hand.

"Do anything for those, won't you? Sit!"

Tarragon obediently sat and received a reward.

"Lie down."

He did and was fed again.

They'd attracted an interested crowd. Huge, hairy black and white bodies surrounded them. What were they doing outside anyway? She was sure most people kept their cows in over the winter. Several cows had their heads lowered as though to charge. Others sniffed and slobbered at Leah and Tarragon. They must have seen her feeding him and wanted the same.

"Shoo, go away. I've got nothing to give you." She flapped her arms. The cows made no move to retreat. "Come on, Tarragon, we'd better make a run for it!"

Leah ran as fast as she could, not daring to look back to see whether the dog or the herd of hungry cows were following.

Leah's borrowed boots and the uneven ground made progress difficult. The rowing machine and stepper down the gym were no preparation for running, terrified, down a steep slope. She'd have to slow down or she'd fall and the cows would trample her. The sight of Tarragon's flapping ears cheered her a little, at least he was safe. After a few more strides she realised the cows, who would be used to moving over uneven grassy surfaces and so could presumably move at least as fast as she, had not butted her or knocked her over. Perhaps after all, they didn't intend any harm.

She looked back to see the cows milling about near where she'd run from. Several had moved a short way as though to follow. Some seemed to be looking at her as though wondering why she'd run. None were chasing her.

"Guess they were just being nosy, eh boy?" she asked Tarragon.

The dog looked at her pocket, but didn't sniff. Obviously he didn't understand her new game so wasn't sure if he'd yet earned another titbit. She gave in and put her hand in her pocket for what was nearly the last one.

Leah tried to take a step toward the dog, but her foot slid out the boot. Hastily she pushed it back in. Looking down she saw she was stuck in very dark mud. The foot of each boot was entirely covered in black gunge. Almost immediately she realised it was also very smelly. Leah bent and grasped the top of one boot and tugged. There was a sucking sound, but the boot didn't come up. She tugged again and almost fell backwards. It was amazing how unstable she felt when she couldn't reposition her feet.

She'd be able to get away, but not with the boots on her feet. The smelly mud looked remarkably cold. She didn't fancy going back in just her socks. Leah tried scrunching her foot into a ball to keep the boot on as she lifted her foot, but all she achieved was to rub the top of her foot and get pins and needles.

Maybe Tarragon could help tug her free? She persuaded him to get close enough for her to attach the lead, then threw a biscuit for him. He lurched forward, jerking the lead out of her hand. The boots hadn't moved and Tarragon had mud an alarmingly long way up his legs. Even if she could make him understand a steady, sustained pulling was required, it seemed possible they'd both become stuck. Sinking two foot into mud was unpleasant for her, it would be far more serious for him. She wasn't prepared to risk that.

Leah checked the mud level and after allowing for it to have splashed about a bit as she struggled, calculated she wasn't still sinking. Maybe Jayne would have some advice, she'd probably got stuck in the mud herself before. Leah fumbled for her mobile and discovered the battery was dead. After a moment's euphoria at the thought Adam might have been trying to reach her and she was unaware, she realised a silent phone wasn't a good thing. Typical. In the city where there were taxis, crowds, police and phone boxes every few feet, she charged her phone every night. In the country where any moment she might be stampeded by marauding cows or get sucked into sinking mud, she drank cowslip wine instead.

She'd got so used to Adam sorting out things like charging her phone, renewing the tax on her car and arranging home insurance she was out the habit of organising her own life.

"Tarragon, go fetch help," she ordered with little enthusiasm.

The dog wagged his tail as though quite willing to take part in any game she liked, just as soon as he figured out the rules.

"Look, doggy, I don't know the right instructions, but if you fetch someone to get me out of here, I'll buy you a whole box of the chewiest and meatiest dog treats on the market."

Tarragon barked once, then rushed past her. Slowly, so as not to risk overbalancing, Leah turned her top half to see where he'd gone. Tarragon bounded in circles around a curly-haired man. The man, who was striding towards her, looked strong enough to lift her to safety. So long as his incredibly large wellies actually fitted him, she was saved.

"Hello," the man greeted her. He seemed amused.

Her heart beat a little faster as she returned his smile. That was just because of the slight danger she was in, or maybe it was just her body's way of telling her she recognised him. She had seen him somewhere before, she was certain. Odd she couldn't think where as he had the kind of impressive physique, cheeky grin and moody good looks it was hard to forget.

"Hi," Leah replied. "Do I know you?"

Chapter 3

The man shrugged. "Tarragon seemed to think you'd like some help getting out of there."

"He's right, I would. Very much." Now help was at hand, she'd stopped panicking and realised the mud was really only a few inches deep. That didn't mean she wasn't grateful to Tarragon for having drawn attention to her plight or for this man having responded.

Tarragon wagged his tail enthusiastically, as though he knew he were being discussed. Perhaps he did. The dog was amazing and this bloke wasn't half bad either, although they were attractive in very different ways.

"Oh! You're the dish..., er, I think I saw you driving a tractor yesterday?"

"Ah. The pink car?"

"Guilty."

They grinned at each other.

"I don't want to seem demanding or anything, but if you're going to rescue me could you do it quite soon? My feet are going numb."

"Right-oh!" He removed his waxed jacket, strode

forward, scooped her into his arms, lifted her gently and stood her on his jacket. Her chilly feet appreciated the warmth from his body retained in the quilted lining.

The dishy tractor driver then extracted her boots and put them next to his jacket.

"They look a bit big. I think that's your problem."

"Yes, I borrowed them from my aunt."

"Best get your own then."

"I don't think I'll be around long enough to need them."

Was it her imagination, or did he look slightly disappointed? Maybe she'd spoken too soon, she didn't have any reason for rushing back to London.

Her legs really were feeling a bit numb so she honestly couldn't help the way she had to cling to him for support as she got her feet back into the boots. He must have understood as he didn't seem at all bothered.

"Are you OK to walk back? I'm not sure I can carry you back to Primrose Cottage, but I could fetch some transport."

"I'll be fine, I think. Thanks for your help."

"No problem. If you like, I could walk part of the way with you, just to make sure you're OK?"

She would like that.

"So how did you get so stuck in the mud?"

'By moving in with a very dull computer nerd' she could have replied, but instead she explained about the cows chasing her.

Her rescuer laughed. "Sorry, I don't mean to be cruel, but I bet you looked funny."

"Maybe, but I was frightened at the time. I hadn't expected to see cows outside in February."

"It's an experiment we're trying at Home Farm. The milkers are kept in, but some beef cattle are hardy and can be kept out all year round. It saves on buildings and bedding and should produce leaner meat."

"I suppose this is the idea of the amazing Mr Gilmore-Bunce?"

"Er, yes. Why do you say that?"

"Sounds typical of him. Letting the poor cows suffer..." She trailed off as she saw his reaction. Ranting at a man she'd only just met and who'd just rescued her wasn't exactly the best way to impress or thank him.

"They're not suffering," he pointed out. "It's more that we're trying a more traditional way of doing things. I do bring them extra food every day. That's where I was going when you passed in your car." He spoke very gently, as though to calm her down.

Leah took a couple of deep breaths. She didn't want to seem crazily biased against his boss as well as hopeless in the face of mud. "Sorry. You're right. I over-reacted." She had good reasons for hating Mr Gilmore-Bunce, but her rescuer presumably saw a different side to him and depended on him for a job. "Are these special cows then?"

"Yes, Belted Galloways are a fairly rare and very hardy breed."

"Funny name."

"It's because of the white stripe around their black bodies."

Leah hadn't stuck around long enough to notice their patterns.

"Oh!"

"What?"

"I have to go back that way."

"I'll protect you - not that you'll need it."

"You don't know what they're like."

"Yes I do. They're very nosy so were checking you out. We don't get many people walking over the footpath."

Leah hadn't exactly been sticking to the footpath anyway, so maybe the cows had a right to wonder what she was playing at.

When they got near the cows, the tractor driver called to them and they wandered over. Thankfully their speed and enthusiasm wasn't a match for Tarragon's. This time she was walking close to the fence so didn't feel so vulnerable to trampling and had remembered that cows are vegetarians. They were still huge though. The tractor driver stroked their necks and scratched the top of their heads which the cows seemed to enjoy. She took his word for the fact that they'd let her do the same if she tried it. He was right, they did look a bit as though they were wearing scruffy white belts.

"So, Jayne Tilbury is your aunt?" he asked.

"Yes."

Were they all psychic in the country? She could handle Jayne knowing more about her than Leah ever said, but it was a bit freaky when a total stranger seemed to have the same ability. He'd known where she was going too. Maybe he'd seen her car in Jayne's yard, but that didn't explain about him guessing their relationship.

"Don't look like that," he said.

"Like what?"

"As though I'm either a psychic or a crazy stalker. I saw you driving to her smallholding, you're out with her dog and you've borrowed her wellies."

Not a mind reader then, just a face reader. Maybe she'd better stop looking at those full lips of his and wondering what they'd feel like to kiss.

"I'm staying with her for a while. A short break, you know?"

"A break from what?"

"London, work, stuff like that." She'd better keep it

simple.

"Maybe I'll see you around then?" he said.

"It's quite possible."

Her heart was beating faster and not just because they were walking uphill. She was surprised to see they'd already reached the stile.

"Yes, well thanks again for your help."

"My pleasure." He definitely looked like he meant that.

Despite her feet which were starting to get sore, she could feel a smile on her face as she walked back. She glanced at her watch, she'd spent half an hour in his company. They hadn't said much; darn it, she hadn't even thought to ask his name! It hadn't been the same as an awkward silence at home though, where she was afraid to speak for fear of saying the wrong thing and starting a row. She'd definitely like to spend more time talking, or otherwise, with him.

She didn't know why she was getting in such a state about him. He was good looking enough, but no more so than Adam. He'd pulled her out of some mud, not saved her life or reputation. It was her idea of a romantic rescue though and what girl wouldn't want to be picked up and whisked away from her problems. That's what she'd wanted from Adam when she'd had her world shattered by her boss accusing her of dishonesty. She'd wanted him to wade in and protest that of course she was innocent, make a fuss, demand an apology from her accusers and then take her away. Ride off into the sunset she supposed. She was hardly being fair. Adam had his own career and reputation to think of and he'd never been the dramatically romantic type.

"Get what you wanted?" Jayne asked as Leah let herself and Tarragon back into the yard.

"I think so. I never made it to the shop though."

"Oh? Sounds as though I'd better put the kettle on for this one."

"And cut a slice of cake. I've had an adventure!"

"Well, tell me," Jayne demanded as soon as she'd poured the tea.

"I've been swept off my feet!"

"What? By a man do you mean, or knocked over by a gust of wind?"

"Both, well I didn't fall over, but he had to rescue me. Jayne, I'm afraid I rather flirted with the dishy tractor driver you told me about. I think it was a sort of reaction to Adam as honestly I'm not usually like that, but he really was gorgeous and he picked me up just as though I was as light as you seem to think I am and he's got such lovely big brown eyes and..."

"Hang on a minute... Dishy tractor driver?"

"You told me about him and I have to admit you were right."

"Sam Cartwright is the estate's tractor driver,"

45

Jayne said slowly, in the same patient voice she'd used to explain things to ten year old Leah during school holidays.

"Well, Sam Cartwright is a dish."

"If you like 67 year old men with faded red beards, then I agree."

"What?" Leah looked at the puzzled expression on Jayne's face. "Oh, Jayne! You didn't lie about the dishy tractor driver too?"

"'Fraid so. You sounded so upset on the phone that I'd have said anything to get you down here."

"So, any idea who my mystery hero is?"

"Yes, but you're not going to like it. It's Oliver Gilmore-Bunce."

"No way."

"Describe him again."

"Getting on for six foot. Gorgeous brown eyes with lashes that'd make even Rosemary jealous, lots of curly hair, strong obviously, but not in a body builder kind of way. Oooh and his voice... sounds like he should be doing voiceovers for some really rich and expensive chocolates."

"Definitely him. Told you he was nice. Just a bit young for me, but I still wouldn't mind being rescued by him."

"No, this guy is a tractor driver, not some pretentious landowner."

"He's not pretentious and he can drive a tractor."

"Sorry, Jayne, but it wasn't your Mr Gilmore-Bunce. I've seen him and he's nothing like my rescuer."

"You sound very sure."

"I am, he was a client of... well, he still is a client of the company I used to work for. He's the reason I had to leave. He isn't as nice as you think he is. Doesn't look as good either, he's older, fatter and shorter and balding. Adam pointed him out to me, but didn't introduce us because he knew he'd be rude, or patronising, or both. He's a sexist pig who wouldn't let a woman handle his accounts until Adam intervened on my behalf. Obviously now, I wish he hadn't but I was regretting it even before the present trouble." Leah's rant eventually ran out of steam in the face of no reaction from Jayne. She lamely added, "I'm very disappointed by your taste in men."

"Hmm, speaking of which, has Adam phoned back about your trouble at work?"

"No. D'you know when I saw my phone was flat I was almost pleased because I could kid myself he'd been trying to call and apologise. Or say he was doing something to help, or even just check I was OK. He's not going to do any of those things, is he?"

"Doesn't sound like it, lovey. No wonder you want a simple tractor driver," Jayne said.

"I don't, I just said he was kind and..."

"Good looking, right. Hmm, but if he's not my landlord, he must be someone new. I'll see what I can find out."

"Not on my account..." Leah started to say, but she had to admit she was curious. It was no more than that really. OK, he'd lifted her out the mud, but Adam had saved her at work. When he'd heard Gilmore-Bunce hadn't wanted Leah to handle his account, Adam had swallowed his own dislike of the man and taken him out to dinner in order to tactfully persuade him to change his mind. He'd even come up with the brilliant idea of having Leah and her client communicate exclusively by e-mail, so she was spared his boorish rudeness and he could pretend that L. J. T. was a man if that's what he wanted.

It rained heavily that night and all the following day. Feeding the sheep, milking Rosemary and collecting the eggs were all much less fun in the wet. The bales of hay soaked up water and were heavier to carry. The mud was deeper making it harder to keep her wellies on.

"Sorry about this," Jayne said as they took a fresh dry bale of straw from the barn and carrying an end each dashed to the pigs with it before the animals' bedding could get wet. The mud splashed up Leah's legs.

"Don't be - these are your trousers, not mine." Leah laughed.

"I didn't really mean the mud. I was thinking of the work you're doing. Your talents are rather wasted on manual labour."

"Talents?"

"You always were a genius at maths and you've got all those finance qualifications. I don't even understand the names of them."

It was true, she did have excellent qualifications. They were what got her into trouble at work. Because of them she'd been involved with the biggest accounts and had access to information that probably would have allowed her to commit the fraud she was accused of. Unfortunately she didn't have the experience she'd have gained if she'd had to work her way up more slowly to such a position of trust, so hadn't spotted when somebody else had tampered with the accounts. Adam had let her down there, by pushing her to accept promotion when she hadn't felt ready. Perhaps because he too had been so impressed with her abilities he'd not foreseen any potential trouble. That proved he wasn't quite so clever himself as he liked to suggest. On the other hand, Jayne was much more astute than she gave herself credit for.

"You're clever too," Leah said. "You know all sorts of things I don't. "

"OK, we're both geniuses! Maybe we'd better put our massive brains to the task of eliminating mud from our lives."

"We can try," Leah agreed. The answer for her was

easy. She could simply return to London. As she looked at the pigs romping around in their fresh, dry straw she wasn't entirely convinced her answer was perfect.

The house smelt of wet dog and drying clothes, both strategically positioned in front of the Aga.

At least, coats, hats and gloves were drying. Some of Jayne's other clothes were getting nearly as wet inside as the ones she wore outside thanks to a leak in the thatched roof. Calmly, Jayne emptied and moved the wardrobe, stuck another load in the washing machine and telephoned her landlord. Leah would have demanded instant action, whereas Jayne made rather light of the situation. Apparently Oliver Gilmore-Bunce promised to deal with the problem at the earliest opportunity.

The following day, Valentine's Day, the rain still poured down, inside and out. Jayne received a card, on the front of which was a very fat cartoon Santa.

"Is the post a bit slow round here?" Leah asked.

"No, why? It's Valentine's Day today, isn't it?"

"Yes, but that's a Christmas card."

"Kind of. My friend Jim sends me a Christmas or Easter or birthday card every year. At least, I suppose it must be him."

"Explain."

"He sent me a Valentine's one when we were at school and I got teased so much I told him not to do it again. Ever since then, I've received a Christmas or other inappropriate type of card on Valentine's Day, so I'm pretty sure he sends them."

"You country people are weird!"

At lunchtime, the women came in to find a single long stemmed red rose lying on the mat in the porch. It was beautifully wrapped in cellophane and lace and tied with a ribbon, but there was no note.

Leah picked it up and carried it in. "You didn't tell Jim he couldn't send flowers, then?"

"No, but I'm pretty sure this isn't from him. The cards are just a joke now and in any case, this isn't his style. Jim doesn't do subtle and mysterious, if he wanted to give me flowers he'd turn up with a big bunch of daisies or something. How about Adam, could he have sent this?" As she spoke, Jayne started to get lunch ready.

Leah knew he hadn't. Worse, she knew he never would. "I really don't think so. If he did, it's the most romantic thing he's ever done."

"He didn't give you flowers?"

"Yes, of course, but there was always a reason. I got a huge bouquet on Valentine's, my birthday, our anniversary, as an apology. This looks a bit more..."

"Romantic, not to mention subtle and mysterious?" Jayne asked.

"Yeah, well one of us has an admirer - unless it's for Tarragon?"

51

"Could be. There's a collie in town who's always very pleased to see him. Come on then, let's eat."

They enjoyed hot tomato soup and toasted cheese sandwiches.

"No one has been round to check up on the roof," Leah complained after they'd eaten.

"What's to check? He knows what the problem is because I told him."

"If someone came round you'd know it was being taken seriously."

"It is being taken seriously. G-B will arrange for someone to fix it as soon as possible."

"You were too soft with him, saying it wasn't a big problem. You should insist something is done right away. People like him get rich by riding roughshod over ordinary people."

"Not him, besides these things take time. He's a good landlord, he'll see it's done right."

Leah wasn't convinced, but clearly Jayne, whilst perfectly capable of running the small farm, wasn't able to deal with the likes of her negligent landlord. Fortunately Leah was; thanks to the way Adam had toughened her up. She could take on the high and mighty Gilmore-Bunce and win this battle - and the one for her own reputation.

The following day the rain eased. Maybe that's what caused the improvement to Leah's mood. Equally it could have been learning the tractor driver was called Duncan. "Actually, he's not just a tractor driver, he's a kind of foreman. And he's not married," Jayne added as though that fact might be of interest to Leah.

"Where do you get your information from?" Leah asked.

Jayne held up the morning's post.

"You wrote and asked someone?"

"No silly. Round here we actually talk to each other instead of doing everything at second hand via e-mails and the like."

"So you asked the postman? That's a good idea, he'd know who'd moved in and what their names were. I'm not sure it was ethical to tell you though."

"Not ethical to know your neighbour's name? How can you welcome them or offer help when it's needed or direct visiting friends who're looking for their new home?"

"Well..." Leah was at a loss. Jayne knew the life history of everyone in Winkleigh Marsh. Leah didn't know the names of all the neighbours in her London flat. When she'd visited as a child she'd never questioned the fact that everyone they met knew not just Jayne's name, but her own and their relationship and what minor mischief they were about to cause. It had been Adam who'd discouraged her habit of making friends at every turn. It was a habit she intended to re-acquire. Quite possibly she'd practice on Dishy Duncan the tractor driver.

Although they still had to wade through mud in the yard, to reach some of the animals, the farm work didn't seem so hard in the sunshine. Leah fed the chickens and cleaned out and refilled their water containers before gathering the eggs. She carried buckets of feed for the pigs and declared herself brave enough to attempt cleaning them out. To her surprise the pens weren't particularly dirty and all Leah had to do was sweep up the mess they'd carefully deposited in a corner away from their bedding. They didn't even smell too bad. Her next task was to fetch a bale of straw to top up their bedding.

Occasionally Leah almost lost one of her boots in the mud, but each time just managed to avoid getting a wet and dirty foot.

"I think I'll get myself a pair of wellies that fit," she said.

"Good idea. I've got to go into town and buy some feed soon, so we could go this afternoon and get you a pair."

Leah decided to buy herself some more suitable clothes too. Jayne's were OK as a temporary measure, but she'd prefer her own. She wasn't sure how long she'd stay this time, but planned to visit far more regularly in future. There was now nothing to stop her coming down whenever she wanted. If she wasn't reinstated at work there'd be nothing to stop her staying permanently. Of course she would be and then she'd be back to her normal busy work schedule and long hours. With a sigh Leah realised that when she wanted to visit Jayne before, it hadn't just been a shortage of time which prevented her, she hadn't liked to risk upsetting Adam by being more insistent that he accompany her and somehow he'd made her feel it wouldn't be a good idea to go alone.

Leah spotted Tarragon on the opposite side of the yard. He seemed to want to cross over to her, but was glaring at the mud which prevented him from doing so while reaching his destination with clean dry paws. After her own experience with a muddy foot she didn't blame him, but couldn't help laughing at the way he'd got himself trapped by picking his way round the edge. Strange that he'd coped better when it was actually raining. With a bark, the dog leapt forward through the mud and bounded towards Leah. She braced herself, but he didn't jump up, just sat calmly by her side and sniffed at her pocket.

"And I thought you'd come to see me, boy, and all you're interested in is what I've got to give you."

Leah didn't have any treats left. "Sorry," she said, pulling out the pocket to prove it was empty. He wagged his tail and slobbered on her hand as though to show he wasn't too disappointed. Maybe she'd misjudged him and he wasn't as shallow as she'd supposed.

"Oh and I promised you a whole box full as a reward for rescuing me, didn't I? I'll get them for you this afternoon."

He wagged his tail again and seemed to grin. Soon it was Leah grinning. A tractor passed the entrance to Jayne's yard and the driver waved to her. She waved back at Duncan and wondered how obvious it would be if she rushed straight into the yard and got herself stuck again. She'd like another opportunity to feel those strong arms around her, but that probably wasn't the best way of achieving it.

Chapter 4

After breakfast, Jayne and Leah cut sprigs of herbs which Jayne tied into neat bunches and packed, with a few drops of water, in plastic boxes. There was rosemary, sage, savory, bay, thyme and mixed bunches.

"The butcher sells these too," Jayne explained. "I wasn't convinced there'd be a demand for them, but when I made the deal for pork and eggs, he asked me to think of anything else he could sell for me. Now I make more profit from these than the meat, especially in the summer when I have a much wider range available."

They loaded the herbs and an unfeasibly large quantity of eggs into the pick-up and took these into the butcher before they started their shopping.

"Thanks, Jayne. Just in time, I've sold out."

"The hens are laying as fast as they can for the time of year, Mike. They should pick up a bit over the next few weeks though."

"Good-oh. And the herbs?"

"Them too. I'll probably have chives and marjoram next week and the mint won't be far behind."

"Good, good. I've been asked for lemon verbena. Do you grow that?"

"No, but probably I could. I'll look into it."

There were several shops selling clothes in town. One supplied outfits for babies and toddlers, another specialised in work wear (steel toe-capped boots, overalls and quilted shirts rather than power suits) there were two charity shops and one that looked as though its customers must only ever go to hunt balls and travelled fifty years back in time to get there.

It was to this last one that Jayne headed. "Don't worry, it's not nearly so bad in the back."

She was right. Once inside, Leah saw a good selection of perfectly normal clothes.

"What's that window display all about?" Leah asked.

"We get a few tourists in the summer and the owners don't like to disappoint them."

"Did I mention that you country people are weird?"

Leah enjoyed trying on comfortable clothes in colours she liked without having to worry what Adam might say.

Jayne said, "Those jeans look a bit baggy. You'd better try a size smaller."

She had a point. The clothes did seem to be more generously cut than the brands she normally wore.

Perhaps she could get away with smaller ones.

"They show off my bum!" she giggled and wiggled as she emerged from the changing room.

"Good, get this too," Jayne said holding up a clingy looking jersey top in bright pink.

"That'll get me noticed," Leah said.

"Good. Dressing like a mouse has encouraged you to act like one."

"I don't," Leah said without conviction. It wasn't entirely true though. Most of her wardrobe had been selected with the aim of avoiding criticism from Adam rather than with any hope of attracting compliments. Most of her actions had, until she drove down to Winkleigh Marsh, been motivated in the same way.

Leah tried on the top. She was right about it getting her noticed. The colour was hard to miss and so she suspected was the amount of cleavage on display. As she looked at herself in the mirror she wished Duncan had seen her in that, with her curves shown off to perfection, rather than covered by one of Jayne's thick anoraks.

She came out and gave a twirl for Jayne.

"Very nice, buy it."

"Oh, I couldn't. It's too low cut."

"Course it isn't, silly. Covers your underwear doesn't it?"

Leah decided to buy it. She doubted she'd have the

nerve to wear it without something over the top, but in this weather she'd need that anyway.

"What about you, Jayne are you getting anything new?"

"Not right now. I prefer to buy things for a particular purpose."

"Me too," she didn't mention she had a purpose in mind and that he drove a big red tractor.

"You'll probably need to replace some of the stuff that got wet when the roof leaked. Will your insurance cover it, because if not your landlord..."

"Leah," Jayne interrupted. "Don't worry about it. There was nothing in that wardrobe that could be damaged by a drop of rain. I keep the few fancy outfits I do have somewhere safe."

"You mean you knew the roof would leak?"

"It's old thatch and an ancient cottage, so it's hardly a surprise."

"If it's not a surprise then there's even more reason for your landlord to have done something about it before now."

"He has. It's been regularly maintained, but thatch doesn't last forever. It's got to the stage of needing to be completely replaced. That's a major job and not that easy to arrange, but I expect it's all in hand. Come on now, we don't want to fall out over G-B do we?"

"No, of course not. He's caused me enough trouble

already." She saw Jayne's face and added, "Sorry."

"What is it with him? I don't understand how you can so dislike someone you've never met."

"You don't like Adam and you've never met him. Maybe it's something that runs in the family?"

Jayne looked thoughtful for a moment, then shrugged. "Maybe. Now, brace yourself, we're going to get the chicken feed next."

"Chicken feed doesn't sound scary."

"It's not, I meant Jim the feed mill's manager. Not that he's scary, he's just... Well, you'll see."

"Is Jim the one who sends the Christmas Valentine cards?"

"Yes."

They put Leah's purchases into the pick-up and drove to the yard to buy chicken feed. First they went into the office and Jayne paid for two sacks of mixed corn, a bag of organic layer pellets and ordered milk powder to be ready for when she got her lambs.

"We pay here, then take the receipt to the mill to collect the feed," she explained.

"Do they sell dog food too?"

"Yes, but Tarragon's got plenty for now."

"I promised him some chews," Leah said. She turned to the lady on the counter. "I'd like the biggest pack of the best dog treats you do."

The woman tapped on her computer. "They're

thirty-two pounds twenty-seven."

"Fine, I'll have them," Leah said. She had no idea how much dog food cost, but thirty odd pounds was a small price to pay for being rescued and introduced to Dishy Duncan.

"You'll have to stay for months now, Leah," Jayne said. "If Tarragon eats that lot this side of midsummer he's going to explode."

They drove round to the mill to collect their purchases.

A forklift appeared and Leah was impressed to see it carried their order.

"Whatever you do, don't giggle, it only encourages him," Jayne said.

Guessing she was referring to the driver, Leah asked, "How did he know what we wanted?"

"Well, out here in the country we have these magic boxes that tell us stuff like that. I think they're called computers. You city types should get them, I'm sure they'd help with keeping your accounts straight too."

Leah could have apologised for having thought everything in the country belonged in the past or even have pointed out that a computer seemed to have done the exact opposite of keeping her and Mr Gilmore-Bunce's accounts straight. She could have if her mind hadn't gone into shock at the sight of Jim throwing his arms around Jayne and lifting her off her feet. As Jayne was squealing and giggling like a schoolgirl it wasn't likely she was aware of Leah's lack of response.

Jim, it had to be him, was well over six feet six. Leah could tell that much by the way Jayne's feet were nearly level with his knees and yet he still had to bend his head to kiss her. That was something he was doing with considerable enthusiasm. Leah couldn't help wishing she had a man who greeted her like that. Maybe she could; Duncan was, she knew, strong enough to lift her off her feet.

Eventually Jim released Jayne and demanded an introduction to Leah.

"Can't kiss a girl, even one as pretty as this, without knowing her name, can I?"

"This is my niece, Leah. Leah, this is Jim."

"I rather thought it might be. Hello, Jim."

Leah, sure no amount of bracing would protect her if Jim really did try to kiss her, offered a hand to shake. Jim took it in his. Although his huge hand completely covered hers, he was very gentle.

"So you girls have been talking about me, have you?" he asked, winking at Leah and keeping hold of her hand.

"Yes and it was all bad, so don't you go getting yourself a big head, Jim Applemore!"

"Too late, Jayne my love. I've got a big everything." He winked again and Leah felt a giggle build up. In an effort not to laugh she looked away from Jim's grinning face, down past her where her hand disappeared into his and right to the ground where she saw the most enormous pair of wellingtons in existence. Even Duncan's would look small next to Jim's. Surely he had to have them specially made?

The giggle escaped. Instantly she was airborne and giddy. Jim had kissed her and set her back down again before she realised he'd picked her up and swung her around just as he'd done with Jayne. Well, it was almost the same. He'd given Jayne a full on snog but contented himself to a loud kiss on each cheek in Leah's case. If anything remotely like this had happened in her office at Prophet Margin she'd have slapped the man's face and filed a report for sexual harassment. This wasn't her office though and Leah was giggling just as Jayne had done. Big as he was, it was impossible to imagine Jim's greeting was anything more than excessively friendly.

Jim loaded the first sack of feed into Jayne's pick-up as though they were no heavier than a loaf of bread. That left two more sacks and a huge box, which Leah guessed must be the milk powder,

"Oh, you'll need this for my order," Leah said, offering her receipt.

"No need, I've got them here." He indicated the box which was bigger than Tarragon himself.

"Oh. Crikey."

"Don't worry, the chews are all in smaller boxes inside, so they'll keep all right. They for Tarragon?"

"Yes, he rescued me, well sort of. Really Duncan rescued me, but Tarragon fetched him."

"Duncan? Now don't break my heart and tell me you've got a boyfriend?"

Leah giggled.

"She means Duncan, Mr Gilmore-Bunce's new foreman," Jayne explained.

"But G-B hasn't..."

"Yes he has," Jayne interrupted. "You don't know what's going on round here."

"Oh, right. I've not met him yet. Nice is he?"

"Yes," Leah admitted and felt herself blush.

"Ah, I see." Jim laughed. "Glad to know a country lad can turn the head of a city girl."

Leah wasn't sure she could explain her head hadn't been turned because she rather suspected it had, so instead she asked why Jim was so sure she was a city girl.

"I can tell you're down from the bright lights of London. Must be because I can see them shining in your eyes. They'd put the stars to shame."

Leah couldn't help it, she burst into giggles again. Jayne was right about that only encouraging him, luckily most of his outrageous compliments were directed at Jayne, but Jim didn't leave Leah out of the conversation.

Jayne mentioned they'd been into town buying

new clothes.

"You don't need them, Jayne you look gorgeous in anything," Jim said.

"Even this?" Jayne indicated the jacket which was probably once waxed and green but was now held together by grease from Rosemary the cow, the sheep's coats, and farmyard grime.

"Absolutely." He caressed her shoulder. "Nice coat this, you know what it feels like?"

"No?" Jayne said.

"Girlfriend material."

Leah giggled again.

"You think I'm corny, don't you?" he asked Leah.

She did a bit, but that didn't mean it wasn't fun to hear his outrageous compliments and she wouldn't at all mind having a man, provided it were the right man, look at her the way Jim was looking at Jayne.

"Well..." She hesitated. Although she didn't want to cause offence by agreeing too easily, neither did she wish to imply she took his every word at face value.

"So would you be if you handled this stuff all day." He pointed to the load of mixed corn on the tines of his forklift. "Suppose we'd better get it into the truck."

He did the job quickly, then kissed both women good bye.

"Nice man, hope I didn't offend him laughing at his chat-up lines," Leah said as they drove home.

"He is nice, far too nice to be offended over someone's amusement. He likes to make people happy."

"He certainly seems to like you and I got the distinct impression he'd like to make you very happy!"

"Oh, he likes me all right, but then Jim likes everybody, at least everybody who's female. I bet he'd even flirt with Rosemary."

Leah could well believe he'd flirt with a Jersey heifer if it'd get a laugh from Jayne, or even provoke jealousy, but that didn't stop her believing Jim had more than a passing interest in Jayne.

"I think there's more to it than that."

"No, lovey there isn't - take it from me. He was flirting with you too, wasn't he?"

"Not like he was with you."

"He doesn't know you as well as he knows me."

And Leah didn't know him well enough to judge how he felt about Jayne. Come to think of it she was rubbish at judging how any man felt about any woman if her relationship with Adam was anything to go by.

Leah had two missed calls on her phone. In London if she'd left it on her desk to go and fetch a coffee she could have that many. Odd how quickly she'd got into the habit of leaving it behind and strange that with only Jayne to talk to instead of constantly checking her e-mails and messages she felt that possibly for the first time in years she was actually communicating.

The first number was Adam's and he'd left a message. The second was that of her colleague Rachel - a text asking her to call. Leah called her first. Cowardly perhaps but she thought it would be easier to listen to what Adam had to say if she had some warning first about how things were at work. She was also curious about why Rachel wanted to speak to her; hopefully not just to gloat over her troubles.

"So what's it like stuck out in the sticks?" Rachel asked. "As dull as I imagine?"

"There's no coffee shop for miles, no broadband signal, a bus twice a day, a couple of pubs but they don't serve cocktails."

"Hell!" Rachel said.

"Actually I'm finding it quite restful, but I expect you'd get bored pretty quickly."

"I'll rest when I'm dead, thanks. Enough of the small talk, I have some good news for you. "

"Tell me."

"The top brass here at Prophet Margin have seen sense over this Gilmore-Bunce fiasco and are going to conduct a proper enquiry."

"Oh good."

"You don't sound very pleased. I assumed it's good news and you haven't decided to make yourself a wood cabin and marry a sheep?"

"No, not that. It's just that they were so quick to suspend me without even giving me a chance to say a word in my own defence and not even letting me back into the building to collect my belongings that I'm not sure they're going to really look into it properly."

"They what? That's dreadful!"

"It is and what's to say the enquiry won't be more of the same? I know how easy it is for a company like that to blame the last one in and hush everything up as quickly as possible."

"Ah, but you don't know who's conducting this enquiry."

"Not Adam Ferrand?" It didn't seem likely that he'd jump to her defence, but she couldn't think who else it could be.

"No, although it's funny you should mention his name in connection with this. It's me, Leah. I'm going to conduct this enquiry and believe me I'm not going to let them blame an innocent party."

There was no doubting the sincerity in the other woman's voice.

"Thank you, Rachel. I, I don't know what to say."

"I like to get my teeth stuck into something and I can just feel there's more to this than meets the eye. At first I thought you'd simply made a mistake or even a series of them and had been hustled out the way to stop you doing more of the same and so they could cover everything up before big investors got wind of it. But if that had been the case I think you'd have been paid off by now. Much better for them to put all the blame on an ex employee than a current one, don't you think?"

"But now you don't think I made a mistake?"

"No, I don't. I'm almost positive that someone deliberately messed up that deal and I'm going to find out who and why. "

"Thank you. I hate to think of anyone believing I'd cheat people who'd put their trust in me."

"Me too. That's why I was so annoyed about the Christmas party."

Rachel was annoyed? It was Leah who'd been given the wrong address and made to look a fool. At least that's what she'd thought at the time. Maybe she'd been too quick to misjudge her?

"Was I wrong, you didn't give the taxi driver the wrong address?"

"No, of course I didn't. Why would I?" Rachel asked. She sounded offended.

"I assumed to keep me out of the way."

"Whoever it was who had you dropped off in a

particularly dodgy part of the city at nine o'clock at night presumably did want you out the way, but I promise you it wasn't me."

Leah believed her. Now she thought about it, if Rachel had done such a thing, she would have just laughed at how successful she'd been, not get upset and deny the accusation.

"Sorry. I shouldn't have been so quick to blame you."

"Water under the bridge, sweetie. Anyway, I did all right for myself without your redhead charms attracting all the attention. I can't prove who caused the trouble that time, but I think it's the same person as has got you involved in this mess, and I'm bloody well going to get him this time!"

Any lingering doubts that her problem wouldn't be properly looked into evaporated.

"Thanks, Rachel. What happens now?"

"I'm going through all the paperwork first. Boring and probably won't help, but it's silly to overlook the obvious. Then I have to get crafty, believe me I can if I need to."

Again, Leah believed her.

"I might as well tell you that Adam Ferrand is involved in this somewhere."

Leah gasped. What did Rachel mean by involved? In the fraud, or in the investigation?

"You'd guessed that hadn't you, that's why you

mentioned him."

"Well..." If Adam was trying to help her, she didn't want to cause trouble for him.

"Can you tell me why?" Rachel asked.

"Not without betraying a confidence."

"OK, I won't ask you to do that now, but if I guess or get told about it, will you confirm it?"

"Yes, I will." It would be a relief to be able to talk to someone about her relationship with Adam and if Rachel found out, it would no longer be a secret. Leah gave Rachel her temporary address at Primrose Cottage; she didn't want it to appear she'd run away.

Leah listened to the message from Adam. He was sorry he'd been so unfriendly on the phone when they'd last spoken.

"I had a lot on my mind, but that's no excuse. You have enough worries of your own and I shouldn't burden you with my problems. Anyway, I hope you're having fun with your aunt. We'll speak soon. By the way, don't forget it's your parents wedding anniversary on the third."

What was that all about? It was almost as though he regretted their split. Sweet of him to remind her about the anniversary too. She was terrible at thinking of buying cards in advance and probably would have left it too late to post one to New Zealand if he hadn't given her a nudge. He'd always been good at keeping her organised in that way. Even though he didn't know the people involved, he understood it was important to her to stay in touch. He'd not met any of her family when they visited London, but he always booked a comfortable hotel room for them, arranged taxis and suggested suitable places for Leah to take them.

Suddenly she missed him and played the message again, just to hear his voice. Was this just another way of manipulating her, or was he simply trying to be nice? Either way it looked as though if she cleared her name she had a chance to get him back - if that's what she wanted.

Chapter 5

Leah awoke in a tangle of sheets, wondering where she was. She'd had a confusing dream where nothing and no one were as they seemed. No doubt because her waking life had the same problems. No, that wasn't right. In real life, her problem was that everything was revealed to be exactly as it appeared. She'd worried her boyfriend was a commitment-phobe who'd not fight for her, that rich and powerful men such as Mr Gilmore-Bunce could ruin her life on a whim and that her employers would drop her rather than lose his business. She'd also known Jayne would welcome and support her and she'd been right. She was right too, in thinking she deserved better than the poor treatment she'd received from the others.

Jayne might be glad of help cleaning out the pigsties but she didn't demand Leah do all the dirty jobs and certainly didn't treat her as though that were all she was capable of.

Leah's work problems could work in her favour. Once her name was cleared, Prophet Margin would have to apologise, admit she was trustworthy and treat her with respect. So would Adam. He'd expected her to always be available to do what he wanted, when he wanted yet never had time for her friends or family. She suspected he'd only agreed to buy the flat with her because he couldn't raise a large enough mortgage himself and not because he really wanted to commit to owning a home with her. If they got back together it would be on her terms. He'd have to acknowledge her at work and he'd definitely have to come with her to Winkleigh Marsh.

She leapt out of bed full of confidence and enthusiasm and dressed in her new pink sweater. In her bedroom it looked even brighter and clingier than it had in the shop. Leah grinned at her reflection as she imagined Adam's expression were he to see her in it. That was the least of what he'd have to get used to. As she trotted down stairs, she was pleased to notice that already her muscles were aching far less than they had after her first day of hard work.

Leah added brown sauce to her plate of sausages and fried eggs.

"Have you milked Rosemary?" she asked.

"Yes, of course."

"Oh, I thought maybe you'd teach me how to do it."

"OK, but your lessons had better be during afternoon milking. I can't see you getting up before six."

Six? Despite having spent over a week on the

small farm, Leah still hadn't realised quite how hard Jayne worked.

After breakfast, Leah changed out of her new clothes and into something suitable for mucking out the pigs. Both she and Jayne received official looking letters. Leah's was from work, politely informing her an enquiry into 'recent events' was under way and her pay would be going into the bank as usual. She'd be checking that later, just to be sure but the tone of the letter reassured her. It said so very little that Leah felt sure they'd taken legal advice and were taking care they didn't seem to be accusing her of anything. It almost implied the 'gardening leave' was at her own request or at least for her own benefit.

She told Jayne the good news. "I'll be able to contribute towards the housekeeping."

"No, I couldn't ask you to do that and things..."

"You're not asking," Leah interrupted. "I'm offering. I know you wouldn't begrudge feeding me if I'd just come up for the weekend, but I've been here longer than that already and I do eat a lot."

Jayne's smile suggested she was too polite to actually say so, but that she agreed with her niece.

"Actually, I would feel more comfortable if I was paying something toward my keep, because I've got a favour to ask."

"Oh dear, that sounds ominous."

"I hope not. If it's OK with you, I'd like to stay for

a while. I think things would be easier with work and Adam if I didn't return to London until my name is definitely cleared and I know exactly where I stand."

"I agree and I'd love you to stay on."

Jayne so obviously meant this that Leah couldn't help but leap up and hug her.

"Was your letter good news?" She asked.

"No, not really."

"Oh sorry. It's just that I thought it might be from some builders to say they were coming to fix the roof."

"No." All the earlier happiness was wiped from Jayne's face.

"He's not going to have it done? That good for nothing... Jayne, what is it?"

"Nothing. Well no, not nothing, but like you I think I'd rather wait until I know exactly where I stand before making a move."

"It's not just the roof, is it?"

"No, not just that. The leaky thatch seems almost too trivial to worry about. Please, let's not talk about it now."

"OK, but when you do want to and if there's anything I can do to help..."

"I know, lovey. Thank you. Just having you here helps. It's good to have family and not to feel so alone."

Leah swallowed. It must have been hard for Jayne to cope with losing both her elderly parents very close together. Leah had been so wrapped up in her new job and new man she'd not been of much help. She'd attended the funerals and written occasionally but that was all. She felt so bad about that, especially compared to Jayne's compassion over Leah's troubles. Now Jayne had something else worrying her, something so bad she couldn't even face talking about it. There was no way Leah could make up for her thoughtlessness in the past, but she could try to ease some of Jayne's present worries.

Jayne had said the leaky thatch was almost too trivial to worry about, but obviously it was still a worry. Maybe it was one problem Leah could help with. Jayne was behaving just as Leah had been at work and in her relationship with Adam - treated badly without sticking up for herself. Unlike Leah who had no one to defend her, Jayne had Leah.

"So, what's the plan today?" Leah asked.

"The usual feeding and cleaning out." Jayne sounded so tired.

No wonder she was tired. It was only eight o'clock and already Jayne had tackled hard physical work before cooking breakfast for her idle townie visitor. Leah offered to do the rest of the morning's tasks and give Jayne a break.

"So, it's just the chickens to be given feed and water and have the eggs collected, the pigs to be fed and cleaned out, the sheep to be fed..." she trailed off. She couldn't do it all before lunch, she couldn't even lift one hay bale on her own.

"I try to think of it as one job at a time, otherwise it's all too daunting," Jayne said, but at least she was smiling again.

"Yes, well I'll start with the chickens."

"Thanks, lovey. Tell you what, you do that and I'll take the pick-up to feed the sheep. I can load up with hay and salt blocks to store in the little shed up there. That'll save me bothering with them at all tomorrow and make feeding them much easier for the next week or so. I've been meaning to do that, but taking the truck means tackling several gates. Sometimes I just don't have the time or energy for things that'd make my life easier."

Leah fed the chickens, an easy task compared to trudging up the field carrying a bale of hay for the sheep and was pleased she was helping to spare Jayne that task for a few days. She'd get her to think of other things they could do to make her life a bit easier. Jayne thought Leah was clever so she'd try to live up to her expectations with a few time and motion improvements. Maybe she didn't need to think of them - just help Jayne find the time to set them in place. Jayne's problem wasn't that she couldn't think of good ways to do things, just that she didn't have the time or energy because she was alone.

As soon as she'd taken in the eggs, Leah mixed up

the pig's feed and gave it to them. As they noisily ate, she swept out their pens, and sprinkled in some fresh straw. Leah remembered how she'd been unable to shift the wheelbarrow last time she'd mucked out the pigs and had to get Jayne to help. She'd learnt her lesson, so this time shovelled only half the dirt into a wheelbarrow and wheeled it to the muck heap, before returning for the rest. Already her muscles were stronger. She didn't find the task easy, but she was able to control the barrow.

Next she checked on Rosemary and Rosepetal. Leah was more than a little relieved to see their bedding was still clean and their hayracks reasonably full. All she needed do was to scoop out a few pieces of straw which had fallen into the younger cow's water trough. Almost immediately, Rosepetal took a look into the trough, shook her head sending another couple of stalks into the water. Then she took a long drink. Leah, remembering Jayne had told her the heifer was pregnant, wondered if this was some kind of bovine craving. She left the straw where it was; even if, as seemed most likely, it's appearance in the trough was accidental, it wasn't going to stop the cow drinking.

"Leah! You've done everything!" Jayne said when she came back.

"I have. Must admit I feel pretty chuffed with myself, so while I'm in a good mood I'll offer to cook lunch while you relax."

"If you're really happy to make lunch, I'll tackle the movement permits and other records. That's another job I've been meaning to get done and one that just gets worse and worse the longer I leave it."

Leah surveyed the well stocked fridge then took a mug of coffee and plate of biscuits into Jayne. "This'll keep you going while I try to figure out that scary cooker of yours."

"Oh thanks, love. Just what I could do with."

"Did you have something in mind for lunch, or shall I surprise you?"

"A surprise would be lovely. It's so long since I had a meal without having to think about what to cook."

Leah didn't want to use anything Jayne might have earmarked for a later meal, so decided to do something based on eggs. Jayne had a plentiful supply of them. There were also home-grown potatoes and plenty of cheese and bacon. Leah made a Spanish omelette, complete with sun dried tomatoes and frozen peas both originally courtesy of Jayne's garden. Never again would Leah moan about the task of trailing round the supermarket to stock her kitchen cupboards. That task was nothing compared to growing and preserving the food for herself.

Leah opened the flue on the Aga and chucked on more dry logs to increase the heat. It took time to peel the potatoes as they were so soft, from having been stored since last autumn, but that gave the cooker time to warm up enough to heat a pan of water. Once the potatoes were on to boil she went outside to pick winter salad. Fortunately Jayne had neatly labelled the rows and she could gather rocket, chicory and land cress. Funny how she'd read those names on imported bagged salad but never known which was which nor realised the crops could be grown in England over winter.

Leah was proud of her omelette, souffled in the oven to a light fluffy texture with a crisp cheesy crust.

"That was absolutely delicious. Thank you, I feel quite spoiled," Jayne said.

"No problem. How did the paperwork go?"

"It's going. I've got things into order now. I think if I crack on I'll get it all sorted today." She sounded as though that would be one less thing to worry about.

"Can I help at all?"

"Not really. It's all hand written notes and forms, and half the information is in my head."

"I'll leave you to get on with it then and I'll go off exploring with Tarragon."

"Take your mobile, then if you get stuck or lost I'll know where to send the tractor driver to rescue you."

"Jayne!"

"Do you mean to say the thought of going over to Home Farm never crossed your mind?"

As Leah fully intended to visit the farm she

couldn't really deny it. The reason wasn't the one Jayne was thinking of, but better to let her believe Leah was planning to flirt with dishy Duncan the tractor driver than that she was going to confront his boss, Mr Gilmore-Bunce about the state of Jayne's roof and his failure to sort it out.

Leah stuffed her pockets with her phone, Tarragon's lead and as many dog treats as she could fit in.

"Come on boy, us country bumpkins are going to leave the wannabe townie to her office work."

Jayne grinned but said nothing.

This time Leah wasn't so frightened of the cows and although she'd have preferred them to display their curiosity at more of a distance she realised their sniffing noses were just checking her out, not wondering how tasty she'd be. Without Leah showing fear for him to react to, the dog barely seemed to notice the larger animals.

Instead of crossing the boggy ground where she'd got stuck a few days earlier, Leah followed the track down towards the farm buildings. If she'd been absolutely sure Duncan would quickly appear to lift her in his strong arms she'd have been tempted to get stuck again. Only tempted though, she knew if she was to attract his attention she'd have to come up with something better than looking a complete idiot every time she saw him.

Once near the yard, she clipped on Tarragon's lead

and walked briskly and purposefully past the various barns and buildings toward the house, with her head held high. She wasn't a trespasser or lost rambler, she was there on a matter of business and with a grievance for which she expected immediate action.

There were several cars parked in the yard. All were coated with more mud than polish and none were new or expensive looking, so must belong to the workers rather than the man himself. G-B's was probably housed in one of the outbuildings. Leah could hear a tractor in the distance and closer was the low hum of some kind of machinery and cattle mooing, but there was no sign of people.

The farmhouse looked like a cross between Jayne's Primrose Cottage and the home of a wealthy landowner. The original building had obviously been extended with a huge conservatory to the right, low outbuildings to the left and a neat glass porch built over the front door. She walked up the uneven red brick path, passing under metal archways covered in ancient looking brown stems. She guessed they'd be covered in flowers later in the year, but couldn't tell which type.

The glass doorway to the porch sported no bell or knocker, so she tapped gently on the glass pane. Immediately she realised the sound was too quiet to be heard by anyone even if they were standing directly behind the solid wooden doorway into the farm house. Leah tried the handle of the porch door.

It opened, allowing a waft of scent to escape. She went inside and pulled the glass door behind her to keep in the relative warmth and the perfume coming from the large pot of blue hyacinths.

Leah pounded the iron knocker onto one of the studs in the wide door. She noticed how much smoother that stud was than all the others and wondered how many generations of visitors had knocked just as she was doing now. After a minute she pounded again and wondered how many generations of tenants and workers had been kept out in the cold, their legitimate concerns ignored by the rich landowners who sat round roaring fires eating lavish dinners or were off chasing poor, innocent foxes.

After ten minutes of banging on the door, walking round outside with Tarragon at heel, first calling 'hello' and then taking a few hasty peeks in at the windows Leah had to admit she wasn't being ignored. There really wasn't anyone in. She took the opportunity to take a closer look at how her enemy lived. None of the curtains were drawn, so that was easy to accomplish. One room was filled with high tech music and entertainment equipment. There was a huge television, speakers everywhere, games consoles - in short every expensive boy toy she could think of. Somehow the large room still looked comfortable. It was clearly an area he used, not just a place to show off the things he could afford to buy.

There was also a beautiful library with big squashy looking chairs placed to receive sunlight at different times of day, strategically positioned lamps and tables and a cabinet stocked with crystal glasses and all types of tempting looking drinks. What bliss it would be to pour a warming drink after a hard day's work and to curl up in one of those chairs with a good book. She craned her neck to see if there was a fireplace. She couldn't see one, but felt sure there would be and that it would be laid ready so a match was all that was needed to supply warmth and the comforting scent of wood smoke. She giggled as she realised that in her daydream she was pouring two drinks as Duncan bent to apply the flame to dry kindling.

Oh well, back to reality. She couldn't confront Mr Gilmore-Bunce but that wasn't his fault so she'd try not to let her anger build against him. She had every right to be angry, but it wouldn't help her try to reason with him and persuade him to fix the roof on Primrose Cottage.

"Come on, Tarragon. We need a plan b."

As she turned to walk back down the path, she saw she wasn't even being ignored - Duncan the tractor driver was watching her. It shouldn't really have surprised her to see him in the yard of the farm where he worked, but she hadn't expected to see anyone other than Gilmore-Bunce.

"Hi, Leah. Can I help with anything?" he asked

pleasantly.

To hide her embarrassment at having been caught snooping and daydreaming of him, Leah demanded, "Where's your rotten good for nothing boss?"

"Who?"

"Oliver Gilmore-Bunce. This is his house isn't it?"

"Yes, it is but he's not actually in there at the moment. What's he done to upset you?"

"It's more what he hasn't done. Fix the leak in Jayne's roof."

"I'll have a word with him." Duncan seemed to be finding this funny.

"He'll listen to a tractor driver?"

Duncan frowned at her for a moment as though he didn't quite understand, then grinned.

"Well maybe if I tug my forelock enough, he'll speak to someone as lowly as me."

"I didn't mean that. It's just he's so pompous. There's nothing wrong with being a tractor driver..." And hadn't Jayne said he was a foreman? Her anger with Gilmore-Bunce had made her be rude - which just made her hate him all the more.

"It's OK, I was teasing. You really don't like Oliver Gilmore-Bunce do you?"

"No. Neither would you if you knew him like I do."

"Oh?"

She could see he was trying not to laugh. Oh dear, he didn't think she knew him intimately did he?

"I work for a company that handles a lot of his investments. Something went wrong with his account and he accused me of fraud and got me the sack."

"You were sacked? That's dreadful. No one has the right to sack you without proof and I just can't believe you were to blame."

Duncan really was sweet. He didn't immediately assume the fault must have been hers and looked sorry that she'd suffered. If it had been him she'd turned to immediately after her boss had told her of his suspicions and suspended her, Duncan would have given her the hug she'd so badly needed.

"Well, I'm not actually sacked, just suspended while they investigate, but my boss did think I was to blame. I'm not so sure what he thinks now."

"Good, well hopefully the investigation will clear your name. Maybe there's been a misunderstanding or there's a reasonable explanation?"

"You're very loyal to him."

"Mr Gilmore-Bunce?"

"Yes. He's the one that accused me and demanded that action be taken."

"If his money was taken then you couldn't expect him to just overlook it."

"Well, no." That was true. She hadn't really thought about it from his point of view. She gathered there were several hundred thousand pounds missing and it was probably natural for him to assume the person handling his account was to blame. He'd put his trust in the company and therefore her, no wonder he was angry and demanding action.

"Leah, is Jayne your father's sister?"

"Yes. Why?"

"I just wondered. Er... Leah, I do have a good reason for seeing things from Mr Gilmore-Bunce's point of view."

"Or you'll lose your job, yes I see. I know what that's like. Sorry I don't want to put you in a difficult position so I'll try not to say anything against that miserable, sexist, snivelling excuse for..." she giggled. "Sorry, I was teasing. Your face though, you looked almost as though it were you I was insulting. I won't be rude about him and won't expect you to be disloyal." She wished she hadn't ranted quite so much about his boss, being so mean didn't exactly put her in a good light. She wasn't even sure she was right. His request to have his accounts checked had, she could see now, been perfectly reasonable, not a deliberate attack on her. Maybe she'd also misinterpreted everything else she'd heard about him.

"So, would you like to tell me what your problem is? Maybe I can help," Duncan said.

She blinked. How could he help with her problems. Then the penny dropped. He meant Jayne's roof.

"The rain. There's nearly as much of it inside Jayne's room as outside. It's worse in some ways as it keeps on dripping after the rain has stopped and it smells awful and stains her clothes and the walls and everything."

"Oh dear. I knew the thatch needed attention, but had no idea the problem was as bad as that."

"No, well you wouldn't. I don't suppose even Gilmore-Bunce does really, because Jayne didn't make much of a fuss. I told her she should have been more assertive."

"Trouble is, there aren't so many people who do thatching anymore. It's not going to be easy to get the thatch replaced quickly."

"I suppose not," she admitted grudgingly. Yet another black mark she'd wrongly put against Gilmore-Bunce. "Actually, flooding in is an exaggeration, but there is a leak in her bedroom and some of her clothes get damp."

"How about covering the roof with a tarpaulin sheet? It'll look awful, but perhaps be better than nothing?"

"Could that be done quickly?"

"Yes, I'll make sure it is."

"Thanks, that's wonderful. Thanks very much, Duncan."

He looked surprised.

Leah blushed. "When you helped me out last time,

I mentioned you to my aunt. She asked around and found out there was a new man who'd started and learnt your name. I'm afraid she's a bit nosy."

"Don't worry, Leah. We're all a bit like that round here," he reassured her. He smiled, but didn't say anything else, so she had no reason to stay.

"Well, thanks again."

As she walked home with Tarragon she realised he'd used her name even though she'd never given it to him. Obviously Jayne wasn't the only one who'd been asking around.

"Here boy," she called Tarragon. "Have some chews."

Chapter 6

A few days later, Leah finished washing up after a late lunch and stood at the kitchen window looking out at Jayne who was standing in the yard as though she were waiting for someone. Leah hoped it was because she could see or hear Duncan coming to fix the roof. Leah rushed back downstairs after changing into more flattering and less smelly clothes, combing her hair, adding another coat of lipgloss and applying mascara, to see Jayne still in the yard.

Assuming Jayne was waiting for Duncan had just been wishful thinking brought on more by her desire to see him she realised. Leah went out to her.

"Jayne, are you OK?"

"What? Oh, yes, yes, of course."

"It's just that you've been stood there for a long time."

"Have I? Yes, sorry I suppose I have. I was just thinking." She gave an unconvincing laugh. "Nothing to do but think around here these days. We've done a brilliant job catching up with all the little jobs that had sort of got missed lately. I'm so glad you're here, lovey."

Despite her smile, it didn't seem that Jayne was completely happy. Leah was sure something was worrying her and guessed the last comment wasn't just because of the work Leah had done.

"Jayne, what's wrong?"

"As we've caught up, I've got time to give you a milking lesson," Jayne said briskly.

Leah allowed her to change the subject. "But you don't usually start until about four."

"No, but I finish by quarter past."

"You think it'll take me nearly two hours to get the hang of it?" Leah asked and gave a mock pout.

"You'll see. Come on." Whatever had been worrying Jayne, she seemed to have put it out of her mind.

Rosemary didn't seem to mind being brought in early for milking and stood quietly eating as Jayne positioned the stool and bucket for Leah. Jayne crouched down by Leah's side and grasped one of Rosemary's teats.

"Put your finger and thumb around the top, like this."

Leah copied Jayne's example.

"You need to squeeze quite hard with the first finger, then gradually curl your other fingers round and squeeze each in turn so you push the milk from the top to the bottom of her teat."

Jayne demonstrated, sending a warm stream of

93

milk gushing into the bucket, then another and another.

Leah tried. Nothing happened.

"Squeeze harder." Jayne showed her again.

"I don't want to hurt her."

"You won't. Remember how hard the orphan lambs sucked on your fingers when you were a kid?"

"Yes. It felt as though they were trying to swallow me whole."

"Well, just imagine how hard a calf would suck."

Leah tried again. A few drops of milk were released.

"Better, but hold really firmly at the top. More of it is going back into her udder than is coming out the end which won't be comfortable for her."

"Sorry, Rosemary," Leah said and had another try. After a few more attempts she managed to create a jet of milk almost as impressive as Jayne managed.

"Yay! I can do it!"

"Keep going."

Jayne worked on two teats simultaneously, while Leah concentrated on the one nearest to her.

Leah continued until her arm began to ache. "This is harder work than I thought," she admitted.

"Harder than you realise. How much milk do you think you've got there?" Jayne nodded towards the bucket.

"About a gallon?"

Jayne blew into the bucket creating a hole in the froth on the top.

"About half a gallon," Leah amended. "How much does she give each day?"

"Four gallons."

"You're going faster than me and doing two at once, so I've managed about a pint?"

"Yes. Well, nearly that much."

"Then for goodness sake, take that food away from her! She's making more, faster than I can get it out of her."

"Don't panic. Once I've got as much as we need, I let the calves in with her and they take the rest."

"We've got nearly enough now, haven't we?" Leah asked hopefully.

"Yes, that's plenty if you've had enough. I give the pigs any that's left over, but they don't really need it."

"I'll just have a quick go doing it two handed, just to see if I can." She could, just about, although the efforts of her left hand produced very little and she couldn't get into a steady rhythm.

"You're doing really well for a first lesson," Jayne assured her.

"A natural, I'd say."

At the sound of Duncan's voice, Leah leapt to her feet, almost knocking over the milk bucket in her surprise. She began the introductions.

Jayne strode over and grabbed Duncan's hand. "Lovely to meet you, I've heard so much about you."

"You have?" He looked confused, but pleased.

"Fancy a cuppa?" Jayne asked.

"Thanks, but I can't stop. I just called in to say we've got hold of the tarpaulin to patch up your roof. I could put it on tomorrow if that's convenient?"

"It is. The afternoon would be best."

"That's fine for me. I'll let you get on with your milking." He nodded at Jayne and winked at Leah. "If I can't find you, I'll know where to look."

Jayne giggled as he walked away.

"It's not funny," Leah said.

"What isn't?"

"He was laughing at how slow I was with the milking."

"You think so? I thought he meant he'd hope to find you in the hay barn."

Leah giggled too. "I don't think so." She sat back on the stool and had another try at milking two-handed. As she squeezed the teats she wondered how long Duncan had been watching and what he'd really thought.

Once Leah felt she'd progressed as well as she could for the first lesson, they let the calves in with Rosemary and took the milk away to strain and chill it.

"Leah, there's something I, er..."

"What?"

"I've got a doctor's appointment tomorrow. It's probably nothing, but I'd got myself into a bit of a state about it."

It didn't seem likely Jayne would get into a state over nothing. "Do you want me to come with you?"

"No," Jayne snapped. She sighed. "Sorry. I'd rather not talk about it, not until I know what exactly is wrong."

"OK." She couldn't force Jayne to confide and didn't want to upset her by trying.

"Besides, I'm going just after lunch and might not be back by the time Duncan arrives. It would look very rude if neither of us was here."

It would a bit, particularly as Jayne had suggested what time he should come. Was that done to distract Leah from worrying about the doctor's appointment, or just a ploy to allow Leah and Duncan to spend some time together? Either Jayne was playing matchmaker, or was desperately concerned about her health - or possibly both.

Leah helped Jayne to bundle up herbs and load eggs into the pick-up before she left for the doctor's. Although they'd already completed all the morning tasks, Leah planned to look busy and competent when Duncan arrived. She filled bags with loose hay in the barn as that was a task she was unlikely to mess up. They looked so soft and comfortable that she was tempted to lie on them for a little rest. She blushed as she wondered what Duncan would think if he arrived to find her sprawled out on the hay and carried the first one over to the lambs' pen just as he arrived.

Attached to the front of the tractor were what looked like the tines from a forklift truck and on them was a huge roll of bright blue plastic.

"Hi, Leah," he called. "I've come to sort out the roof. Jayne about?"

"No, she's gone to the doctor's."

"Jayne? I've never known her to be ill."

"Never?" How long had he been working at Home Farm? Three, four weeks?

He looked embarrassed. Maybe he'd done so much asking around about her, he felt as though he knew them both better than he did? That made her want to rescue him from his discomfort.

"I know what you mean though, she doesn't seem the sort to get ill, does she? It's just a routine check thing though, nothing to worry about," she added, hoping it was true.

"That's good. If you're willing to give me a hand, we can get the roof patched up before she comes back."

"I can try, what would I have to do?"

"Just work the hydraulics on the tractor to lift me and the tarpaulin up onto the roof." He pointed at the blue plastic.

"Hydraulics?"

"You just push a lever, it's easier than changing gear in a car. Come on, I'll show you."

She climbed up into the tractor cab and sat in the seat. Tarragon tried to follow.

"I think I'd better put him inside, I don't think he'll be much help."

She took the dog into the cottage and came straight back to resume her seat in the tractor.

Duncan stood on the step and showed her how to raise and lower the forks. The levers did look rather like a gear stick and just had to be pushed forward or back.

"Do it very slowly, if it jerks too much I'll fall off. As it goes up, use this one here to keep them level."

"I'd better practice before you get on."

"Go on then."

She could have found the right lever and pushed it in the correct direction without him taking her hand and guiding it, but she didn't like to say so. His touch was warm and gentle and she felt a thrill that wasn't entirely due to managing to control the unfamiliar equipment.

Her first efforts to raise and lower the forks were a bit jerky, but she soon managed to manoeuvre them reasonably smoothly.

"Excellent. Now this one," he lifted her hand onto a third lever, "is to slide the forks out. You'll need to do that once I'm up above the roof."

"You're going right up there?"

"That's where the hole is."

A good point, but it seemed awfully high and rather dangerous if he had to rely on her to raise him safely.

She practised using all three levers until she was sure she could manage.

"That's it, you've got the hang of it. If you make a mistake when I'm up there, don't panic, just let go of everything and either wait until you remember what to do, or yell to me for instructions, OK?"

"Got it."

"Great. We just need to get the tractor into position. Scoot over a bit and I'll move it forward."

He slid onto the seat beside her and put his arm round her to grip the wheel.

"Ready?"

She was more than ready.

He touched her leg to indicate she was to use the clutch. The tractor crawled forward. She was impressed it could go so slowly, especially as she was in no hurry to get there which would mean she'd no longer be able to lean back against his chest with his arm wrapped around her or feel the warmth of his thigh pressed against hers.

Leah looked down at the gear lever. "Crikey, how many gears has this thing got?"

"Eleven forward and four reverse in both upper and lower ratios. It's in the lower ratio now and on flat ground like this it could easily pull away in sixth."

"This is sixth gear?" Surely if it were moving any slower it would be stopped?

"No, first." Obviously he wasn't in any more of a hurry than she was.

Once the tractor was close enough, Duncan jumped down. "Just do exactly what you practised. I'll point up or down to show you what I want."

"I'll try to get you in exactly the right position."

"Sounds fun." He winked at her, then jumped down and climbed onto the roll of blue tarpaulin.

Duncan gave her a thumbs up. She smiled and returned the gesture before realising he was probably indicating for her to lift him up. She put her hand on the lever and pulled gently. The forks and Duncan rose slowly. She noticed she'd have to straighten him up at just the point he held out a hand and wobbled it to indicate that's what he wanted her to do.

Leah found it easy to interpret Duncan's hand

signals and translate them into the appropriate movements of the levers. She did feel a little nervous when he was above the cottage roof and she had to extend the forks. He looked vulnerable and was trusting her not to let him fall.

Once in position, Duncan climbed out onto the tines and began opening up the tarpaulin. He looked perilously unbalanced as he hefted the heavy material and turned it over. Just as she thought he'd set himself an impossible task, he threw the sheet. It landed perfectly in position. Duncan indicated for her to retract the forks.

In her impatience to get him safely back down she jerked the lever causing Duncan to lose his footing. She was sure he'd fall and raised her hands to her face. When she looked again he was still on the forks, kneeling now and with his arms at full stretch reaching for the metal supports, but still there. Still safe.

Leah had to take several deep breaths before she dared touch the controls again. By that time, Duncan had slithered back along the tines and braced himself more securely against the framework. Slowly she reached for the lever and eased it ever so gently. Getting him back down seemed to take much longer than it had to lift him up, but eventually he was back on the ground.

She jumped down from the cab and ran to hug him. "I'm so sorry, I thought I'd dropped you."

"It's OK, I'm fine," he whispered in her ear. The feel of his arms around her and the warmth of his breath did nothing to calm her heart rate.

"My fault, I should have warned you that without the weight of the tarpaulin, the hydraulics might work more quickly."

It was nice of him to say that, but she knew the mistake was hers.

"Come in and have a cup of tea or something. I know I could do with one and I wasn't the one in danger or having to do all the hard work."

"A cup of tea would be nice," he said. "I'd better tie the tarpaulin down first. I don't want it flying away before I've finished the job."

He used ropes attached to eyelets in the corners of the blue plastic sheet, to fix it securely in place.

Tarragon greeted them both as though he hadn't seen them for weeks and had spent every moment looking forward to being able to slobber on them and bash them with his waggy tail. Because of that, they had to catch hold of each other for support as they removed their coats and muddy boots. Or at least, that's the excuse Leah would have used if he'd asked why she had her arm around him.

"Go in there and take a seat," she said gesturing in the right direction.

Leah made them both a cup of tea and took it into the living room where he was sprawled on one sofa.

He'd positioned himself at one end so there was plenty of room for her to sit next to him. She wasn't sure if that was an invitation or if he just thought it was easiest to sit near a table on which he could put his mug. She handed him his tea then sat on a chair where she could watch him. Immediately she jumped up again.

"Are you hungry? We've got cake, or I could make you a sandwich?"

"What kind of cake?"

"Dundee. Jayne made it."

"Go on then, you've talked me into it."

As she cut the cake she remembered his arm around her as he'd driven the tractor. Whether his choice of seat was intended as an invitation or not, he wasn't going to mind her sitting next to him.

He didn't react when she returned with his cake and sat beside him, but Tarragon did. He came over and placed his head between them. They both went to stroke him at the same time and Leah ended up holding Duncan's hand rather than Tarragon's silky ear. She was almost sure that had been completely accidental. Duncan grinned at her but said nothing, even when she felt herself blush.

"So, have you always been able to drive a tractor?" she asked, grabbing at the first subject of conversation that occurred to her. It was hardly brilliant as presumably his feet wouldn't have reached the pedals during his early years.

"Pretty much, yes. My dad taught me when I was a kid. He sat me on his lap and let me steer."

So, she wasn't quite such a blithering idiot as she'd feared.

"And you've never learnt despite having an aunt who's a farmer?" he asked.

"No. When I came here as a kid Granddad, Jayne's father, still drove the old tractor and I was too small then. It was a funny little thing with no cab and absolutely no safety features. I never wanted to try though, I was just interested in the animals, especially the orphan lambs."

"I used to love feeding them when I was a kid. We don't bother with them now on Home Farm, but I think every farming family has a few when there are children about."

"I used to feed them whenever I came here. They were so cute. I'm glad I never believed Jayne when she used to tell me they'd end up on the dinner table."

"You didn't know?"

"No. Proper little townie I was. She used to tease me something rotten."

"I bet! I had townie cousins who used to visit in the holidays, so I can imagine the stunts she pulled."

Their tea was drunk and refilled as they laughed over childhood memories that whilst not shared, felt as though they were. It wasn't until he was laughing about the time Jayne convinced her that she'd got ringworm and all her hair would fall out that Leah wondered why Jayne was still not back and checked the time.

"Crikey, we've been chatting for an hour. I hope you're not going to get in trouble with your boss?"

"What? Oh, no don't worry. Leah, about that..."

Duncan was interrupted by a loud yap from Tarragon who began spinning round in circles.

"Jayne must be back," Leah said rather unnecessarily.

"Looks that way. Leah, would you like to come out tonight?"

Leah didn't know how to respond. She'd have loved to say yes, but as Jayne had been at the doctor's for so long there must be something wrong. She couldn't go off out leaving her aunt worried and alone.

"Just a drink. No pressure," Duncan coaxed.

"I can't really. Jayne's well, she might want to talk and..." She trailed off. She'd be going back to London soon, was starting a relationship down here a good idea? She'd had enough of half truths and people not saying what they really meant to last a lifetime. She owed it to herself to be completely honest.

"Well, maybe another time?"

"Maybe, but it would just be as friends. I'll be

living back in London soon."

"Oh, I see." He didn't sound as though he did.

Fortunately, Jayne came in before the atmosphere became too uncomfortable.

"Thanks for patching up the roof, looks like that should solve the problem," Jayne said.

"Temporarily anyway. Sorry it looks such an eyesore, but hopefully it won't be for long."

Excellent, Leah thought. Duncan wouldn't be reporting to G-B that the job was done and dusted, but would remind him that a complete re-thatch still needed to be carried out.

"Well, I'd best be off." Duncan was already half way across the room as he said that.

"I'll put the kettle on," Leah told Jayne. She needed time to think.

"Make mine Camomile tea, please," Jayne said, naming the herb she'd said was good for relaxation.

Leah already regretted saying no to Duncan. He'd only asked her out for a friendly drink and, hard though it was to get used to the idea, she was now single. It was time she admitted to herself that it was all over between her and Adam. Had really been over even before she'd been accused of fraud. Long before that she'd been unhappy and their relationship had been in a rut. Stuck in the mud and yet when a man offered to pull her out again she'd said no.

Leah fussed over Jayne, getting her to sit down and

bringing her tea and cake.

"So, how did it go at the doctor's, or don't you want to talk about it?"

"Oh, it's fine. I'm maybe going to have to go in for them to check something out but it's nothing to worry about."

"Oh good, I was worried." She still was.

"I told you not to be."

"I know, but you were gone so long."

Jayne burst out laughing. "No, I wasn't! I came back just in time to see you dragging that poor man into the cottage, so I thought I'd hang about outside for a while. I hope it was worth me getting cold for?"

"Jayne! I didn't force him to come in and we drank tea, that's all."

"He didn't ask you out?"

"Well, yes he did."

Jayne put down her mug of tea and leant forward. "Where are you going and when?"

"We're not. I said no."

"Idiot."

Leah sighed. "Yes, I think maybe you're right."

"I know I am. Remember I told you about Jim and the Valentine's card?"

"Yes. Why didn't you ever go out with him?"

"Because, like you, I was an idiot. He asked me a few times and I said no. He asked someone else and she said yes. They got married. End of story."

"But he's not married now?"

"No, but... will you stop changing the subject when I'm trying to lecture you? My point is, don't say no if you want to say yes."

"Advice you'll be taking if Jim asks you again?"

Jayne put her hand to her ear and then shook her head as though she'd not heard. "I hope that's the only invitation you're going to turn down?"

"I'm not sure he'll ask me again." Leah consoled herself with a slice of cake.

"Oh dear. Still, that wasn't quite what I was thinking about. Do you remember my friend Chantelle?"

"The arty type who lives in the water-mill? I remember. She was a little crazy but a lot of fun. Didn't she stick up for me once when you were teasing me about my braces?"

"That's her. She never liked anyone to be picked on for their appearance. People used to laugh at the way she always made her own clothes, but not anymore."

"She's got good at it?" Leah guessed.

"I'll say. She's actually a clothes designer and doing quite well. She's had that mill properly converted and now has fabulous parties there. Lots of her friends are well known; musicians, chefs, artists and she ropes them all in to help. She's throwing another one and we're both invited."

"Sounds like fun."

"It will be. There'll be romantic lighting and dancing and fine wines and Duncan will be invited."

"Sounds like a whole lot of fun."

Chapter 7

Leah phoned Adam from her bedroom at Primrose Cottage.

"What do you want? I'm very busy."

"I wondered if you knew how the investigation at Prophet Margin was going? I had a letter saying I was suspended while..."

He cut her off. "I can't possibly discuss this with you. Surely you realise it's official company business?"

He must know Rachel was investigating the matter; why was he so reluctant to reassure her that she'd soon be found innocent?

"I can't see why that means you can't talk to me about it. I just want to know who's investigating what and how long it might take. Whose business is it if it's not mine?"

"Be reasonable, Leah and try to look at things from someone else's point of view for a change. Things are rather awkward for me over this trouble."

How dare he? She'd always tried to see things from his point of view. She was trying now, but she still couldn't see why, when she was the one suspended through no fault of her own, it was him who felt hard done by. She could only think of one reason - he thought she was guilty. He'd never trusted her, that's why he'd been so controlling about where she went, which friends she had and was so insistent about the prenuptial agreement.

"Sorry to have bothered you." She ended the call and rang Rachel's number. Leah wasn't sure why as she wouldn't be able to tell her anything, especially as Leah only had her works number and even if she was willing to talk then she might not want to be overheard doing so.

"Oh hi, Leah I was just about to call you," Rachel said.

"Really?"

Rachel laughed. "That never sounds convincing does it? Sort of thing estate agents and the like say when they've been keeping you in the dark for days and you've finally managed to track them down."

"But in this case, you haven't been keeping me in the dark?" Leah tried not to sound sarcastic, there was no point in antagonising someone who potentially could help her.

"Only because there's nothing to tell, or at least there wasn't until a short time ago."

"And now there is?"

"Yes, sort of. We had a call from Mr Gilmore-Bunce recently. Somehow he'd heard there was a problem with his account and offered every assistance in helping to sort it out."

"But he was the one who raised the issue and had me suspended!"

"No, no. The suspension is simply company policy whenever there's any sort of... well, if there's any irregularity..."

"There's no need to be delicate, I know I'm suspected of stealing all his money. What I don't understand is who made the complaint if it wasn't him."

Rachel didn't reply.

"You can't tell me?"

"No. I don't know for sure and I wouldn't want to make an accusation without proof."

"But someone has done - about me?"

"It would seem so," Rachel agreed. "We'll get it cleared up though, Leah, I promise."

"You do sound more positive about that."

"Yes. I wouldn't have let you, or anyone else, take the blame without proof, but I wasn't sure that we'd find the truth. I worried Prophet Margin might try to hide it from the investor."

"Gilmore-Bunce?" Leah interrupted.

"Yes, but as he already knows they can't hope to do that. He's offered access to any of his records that might help which will make things much easier."

"Great news. Thanks, Rachel."

Leah sat on her bed, trying to recall what her boss had said when he'd suspended her. It was difficult to remember as she'd been so shocked and upset. Perhaps he hadn't said who'd accused her and she'd just jumped to the conclusion it must be Mr Gilmore-Bunce because there had been so many transactions on his account and as Adam had said, he had a reputation for being unreasonable. If it had been Leah who'd first mentioned the investor's name it wasn't quite so surprising her boss had thought there might be some truth in the allegations. She sighed; she really had misjudged G-B. Thank goodness he'd never know her opinion of him.

"Are you all right up there?" Jayne called.

"Fine, just coming down."

She explained about her phone call with Rachel. "I used to think she didn't like me, but we've put that behind us and I'm sure she won't let it influence her investigation."

"Actually it might. She'll probably be extra thorough to make sure she's not seen to be biased against you."

"Maybe. So, what's the plan for this morning?"

"I'm digging a trench for the runner beans. It's hard work that would be easier with two."

"All right, you've talked me into it."

Jayne dug the trench as Leah fetched barrow loads

of compost to fill it up again. Then Jayne heaped the excavated soil back on top.

"It looks like a grave for someone very tall," Leah said.

"Hmm, anyone particular you want to bury in here, then?"

"If Adam had been here when I spoke to him this morning, I'd have been quite tempted to push him in, I have to admit."

"You go get him, I'll whack him with the spade," Jayne offered.

"Jayne! I just meant push him in and chuck compost at him. I was really annoyed, but it's probably my fault. I seem to have been jumping to the wrong conclusions a lot lately."

"If he annoyed you, I expect the fault was his."

"I don't know..."

"Anyway, we have more important matters to worry about. What shall we have for lunch?"

They decided on a plate of cheesy-hammy-eggies accompanied with a green salad. Leah didn't like to admit she didn't know what a cheesy-hammy-eggy was, but guessed there was a clue or three in the name.

"I'll pick some salad, shall I?" she suggested.

Leah thought Jayne was right about Adam being to blame for annoying her earlier, but she felt she should give him the benefit of the doubt and rang his mobile to see if an apology could return them to more friendly terms.

"Leah, didn't I say not to ring me at work?" he snapped.

"Isn't this your lunch break?"

"Yes," he answered, reluctantly.

"So it's not in work's time nor on the premises - unless you're still at your desk trying to clear my name?"

"Exactly and I'll do it much better without interruptions."

He'd do it better without people around him ordering cappuccinos and panini too, but Leah didn't mention what she could hear in the background.

Adam was lying to her but she didn't know why. He seemed even more irritable than usual whilst Rachel, a colleague who'd never liked her much, was full of enthusiasm at the thought of clearing Leah's name. It was almost as though Adam wanted her to be in trouble - perhaps as an excuse to break up with her. Fine with her. Now she was sure where she stood with him and could try to move on from the relationship. She thought she might be able to think of someone who could help her with that.

As she gathered rocket and mizuna leaves, Leah felt strangely relieved. Jayne noticed a change in her when Leah brought in the salad to wash.

"Been thinking things through?"

"Sort of. I called Adam again. I'm beginning to wonder what I ever saw in him."

"You OK?" Jayne asked.

"Yeah. I think so."

Jayne continued to look thoughtful. Then she brightened, held up a finger to suggest she'd thought of something clever and said, "Plenty more turnips in the field."

"Nice, I've always wanted a dirty boyfriend with orange flesh, purple skin and green hair."

"You're thinking of swedes."

"An enigmatic blond? Now you're talking!"

Both women giggled together as they finished preparing the meal. Silly schoolgirl humour had cheered Leah much more than sympathy would have done.

Cheesy-hammy-eggies were Jayne's version of croque monsieur; cheese and ham sandwiches, dipped in a mixture of eggs, mustard and seasoning, then fried until crisp and golden on the outside. As Leah cut into hers, the gooey melted cheese oozed onto her plate. The rich snack contrasted wonderfully with the tangy plain salad and helped Leah feel better still.

She decided to concentrate on something positive and thought about what to wear to Chantelle's party. She could never hope to compete with the hostess of course, especially if she wore one of her own creations. Leah had heard of Chantelle Miller the designer but hadn't realised she was Jayne's old school friend.

When they went food shopping that afternoon, Leah leafed through a couple of copies of celebrity worshipping magazines and sure enough, many of the catwalk frocks were Chantelle's creations. Her thoughts of clothes were temporarily forgotten though when Jayne began filling the trolley. She didn't seem to buy anything Leah recognised as food.

"Right, what do we need?" Jayne asked.

"Cakes and biscuits, obviously."

Jayne selected flour, cocoa and sugar in place of the chocolate cake Leah would have opted for. She bought golden syrup and rolled oats rather than a pack of flapjack squares.

"That steak pie you gave me the first day I was here was delicious."

"I'll make another, there'll be enough flour left over for that."

"Do you buy butter, or make it?"

"I made a batch soon after Rosemary calved, as she had so much milk then. It's hard work and only worth doing if you're making a lot, so I do the biggest batch I can and freeze it. It's nearly all gone now though."

Considering how much the two of them ate, Jayne didn't seem to have bought much.

"Jayne, I meant what I said about paying my way. If you want more stuff..." Leah trailed off when she saw Jayne laughing.

"Don't worry, lovey. I won't starve you. We've got meat, milk, eggs and plenty of vegetables from the farm, so really I don't need to buy that much."

"Even so, I'd like to pay towards my keep."

"All right. Pay me something if it makes you feel more comfortable, but not too much or I'll be the one who's not happy."

Leah smiled. She knew Jayne kept a jug containing a small amount of 'emergency cash' on the sideboard. She'd put her housekeeping contribution in that to save them both any embarrassment.

Once they'd got home, put the shopping away and had a cup of tea and piece of cake, Leah had another go at milking Rosemary. Jayne got her started, then left her to get as much milk as she could before her arms ached.

The rhythmic action of squeezing and releasing the cow's teats was quite soothing and Leah found her mind wandering from the task, to the forthcoming party. In particular, she thought about the only other person she knew would be on the guest list; Duncan. She needed to find a way to let him know her return to London wasn't going to be happening soon. She also needed to make a good impression so that he'd welcome that news.

Leah thought something plain and simple might be best both for her and for Jayne. That way they wouldn't get it spectacularly wrong. She'd learnt the hard way that dressing to impress rarely worked. All she had to do was convince Jayne that more clothes shopping was a good idea.

When she took in the strained milk she asked Jayne if there was anything special they had to do the following day.

"It's Chantelle's party. You hadn't forgotten?"

"I meant in the day beforehand. Other than the usual milking and feeding, I mean."

"No, we're pretty much caught up with everything."

"Good, then I'd like a bit of retail therapy. I want to buy dresses. One for each of us for Chantelle's party."

Jayne shook her head. "I don't need a new dress."

"I never said you needed one, just that I was going to buy you one."

"Well, I don't..."

"Oh please. I want to forget all about rotten Adam and have fun and you did say Duncan was invited?"

"Yes, he's going all right."

Leah could see her plan was working. "I want to look really nice, but I'll feel silly if I'm all dressed up and you don't have a new dress."

"Hmm, doesn't look like I've got a choice, does it?" Jayne said. She didn't look as annoyed as her words suggested.

"None at all."

Jayne picked out a simple white shift dress for Leah.

"You'd look stunning in that."

Leah tried it on. Stunning was an exaggeration, but she thought it suited her much better than the super stylish clothes Adam had thought were appropriate. So often she'd walked into a function and seen someone slimmer and more confident in the same outfit.

Jayne's own choice, when pressed to try something on, was similar, but longer and black. It suited her very well.

"I'll take both," Leah told the assistant and she'd paid before Jayne got back into her own clothes and was able to raise any objection.

Jayne did the evening milking whilst Leah shut up the chickens and had a quick bath. She guessed correctly that she'd need longer to do her hair and make up than Jayne would want to spend on hers.

They both wore silk scarves made by Chantelle. Leah's was grey and purple which brought out the blue of her eyes. Jayne's was a soft green to contrast with her red hair.

It was surprising how much alike the two women

looked, despite the differences in their age and lifestyles. Jayne had always worked hard, only leaving the farm to go to college and even then she'd studied agriculture.

Leah, on the other hand had it easy. Her father was a diplomat, so Leah had attended an expensive English boarding school and spent her holidays with her parents in various exotic locations, or in Winkleigh Marsh with her grandparents and Jayne.

Seeing Jayne's eyes sparkle at the prospect of the party made Leah realise how strained she'd looked over the last few days. Now she looked so young and happy.

"We look pretty good, I think?" Jayne said as they admired themselves in the long mirror.

"We do. The fresh air and exercise have done me a world of good. You'd already said I don't look plain and fat anymore, now I don't even feel it."

"I should hope not! You never were plain or fat, even when you had those braces you were beautiful. Who on earth told you different?"

"No one," Leah said truthfully. He'd never actually said it, but somehow Adam had made her feel that way.

"Hmm. You can talk to me, you know."

"Yes, I do know." Leah hugged Jayne. "I reckon we could tell each other anything."

"Of course we could, lovey."

"So what is it that the doctor told you to take the spring out your step?"

Jayne gasped, then grinned. "How did you manoeuvre me into that, you crafty cow?"

"I used your own techniques against you. Now spill."

"All right, I am worried about my health. And you're right, I should talk about it. Not now though, eh? The taxi will be here any minute."

"Well..."

"Come on, lovey. We'll talk about it tomorrow and you can be properly sympathetic, but we'll enjoy the party first."

"All right."

Jayne hugged her again. "Thanks, lovey. I expect I've been getting myself into a state over nothing. I feel better just to know I've got you to share this with. I knew I had, I just didn't like to say because... well, tomorrow?"

Leah had been at the party for thirty seconds before realising she'd been right about their clothing. There were plenty of beautiful, but stick thin, women in dresses that obviously cost more than Leah earned in a month. They didn't look particularly comfortable. There were also other people, some of whom Leah recognised as being local, who were dressed as though they were there to have a good time. Glancing round, Leah could see that the party was designed for fun, not for a good write up in Hello! or to make other people's efforts at entertainment look inferior.

The drinks, which were Elderflower champagne, local beer and fruit cup, were packed into cages and lowered into the icy cold mill water. In the courtyard garden a hog roast was set up. The fire from that warmed the outside space. Real fires were also lit inside the mill. The height of the room and the curved wooden beams gave the appearance of a cosy cathedral. The decorations were huge tubs of greenery and twigs with coloured bark. Higher up were draped lengths of printed silk. These were mostly of the same soft green as Jayne's scarf, or in the mauves and greys of Leah's so the women felt they fitted in perfectly.

There were huge glass dishes of classy salads, a huge chocolate cake and a mountain of fresh fruit.

The music was provided by a series of live bands and singers. Leah recognised many of the songs from the radio and television. It took her a while to realise the singers were familiar too and the entertainers weren't simply covering the songs of famous artists.

The first part of the evening was taken up with looking round Chantelle's interesting home, being introduced to numerous people - both local and famous, and with eating. Duncan greeted her more enthusiastically than she'd expected after she'd turned down his offer of a drink. It was good to know he wasn't the sort to hold a grudge and could be friendly with her even if she wasn't offering anything else. She wasted no time in trying to explain she'd been abrupt before because she'd just come out of a relationship with someone in London. If she was a little clumsy about working that into the conversation, it didn't seem to bother Duncan.

"I don't suppose you'll be single long, so I'd better move fast. Can I fetch you a drink?"

He returned with a glass of the aromatic sparkling wine, but was soon claimed by an elderly lady. She seemed confused but there was no denying her intention of speaking to him. He shrugged.

"Excuse me, Leah. I'd better give in gracefully." He led the lady away to a quiet corner.

Duncan reappeared at her side at frequent intervals, each time bringing her another glass of the elderflower drink and each time being dragged away again by various friends after just a few words. Leah was a little disappointed not to chat to him for longer but she couldn't complain she was short of company. There were plenty of other people wanting to chat and flirt with her and Jayne. Jim was the only one who got much of a chance. Dressed in a smart shirt and trousers instead of dusty overalls he looked quite respectable. That didn't make him behave any better than he had done at the feed mill though.

When Leah remarked on the number of people present, Jim looked puzzled.

"I see only two people, but they are so beautiful I don't want to look at anyone else." That, of course, provided him with another excuse to kiss Jayne and Leah. And then Jayne again.

The delicious wine went to Leah's head and she took it in turns with Jayne to flirt with Jim and anyone else who joined their small circle. She knew she was acting a little silly but it was great to get a reaction, from a man, that was something other than a disapproving frown. The old lady who'd claimed Duncan earlier in the evening tapped Leah's elbow and beckoned her to follow

Leah, following into a quiet corner, wondered if she'd have to endure a lecture about unladylike behaviour. Instead the lady wanted to tell her what a dear boy Ollie was. It took Leah a minute to realise she meant Duncan. Once she did, she agreed enthusiastically. Perhaps too enthusiastically because the lady beamed and said how nice it was that something was going right for him after all his problems. She seemed to assume the two of them would naturally get together. Leah hoped she was right about that, though glad she was wrong about the name. Ollie was a silly name, probably short for Oliver.

The glass fell from her hand and shattered. People rushed to clear it up, but Leah couldn't move. Jayne had told her Duncan was Oliver Gilmore-Bunce and Leah hadn't believed it. Adam had pointed out an

126

older, far less attractive man and said he was G-B and she'd believed him instead - just as she'd believed all the awful things Adam had said about the man. They hadn't all been true, she had since realised, maybe his identification had been no more accurate. If Duncan was G-B, what did that mean? He said he didn't believe she'd committed the fraud, but then he'd said he was Duncan...

"Are you all right, dear?" the old lady asked.

Leah couldn't reply.

"Anyone know where May is? Her girl looks like she's had a bit of a shock."

May? That was her grandmother's name. The lady was confusing Leah with her aunt. Duncan was just Duncan and this sweet old lady was just terrible with names. Leah took a deep breath.

"Want to sit down?" the old lady asked.

"No, I'm fine really," Leah reassured her. To prove it, she escorted her new friend to the buffet table where they both managed a few more mouthfuls of delicious roast pork and spiced apple sauce.

Later, the music became softer and the mood more romantic. Jim approached Jayne and Leah holding a hand over one eye.

"Are you OK?" Leah asked.

Jim removed the hand and stuck his fingers in his ears. "Too much loveliness at once confuses a poor chap like me. I've got to pretend there's just one of you or I'll go crazy deciding which one to dance with first."

Leah stood behind Jayne. "Does this help?"

"Indeed it does. Jayne, please dance with me?"

Jayne looked at Leah who'd just caught sight of Duncan approaching, this time without a glass in his hand.

"Go on, Jayne, I'll be fine."

Duncan came close enough to whisper, "Shall we?" as he gestured to the dance floor.

Leah nodded and stepped into his arms.

As soon as he slipped his arm around her waist and pulled her close, she knew that was what she'd been waiting for all evening.

He didn't speak as they danced, just held her gently and moved slowly in time to the music. She felt ridiculously happy as though nothing in her life could ever go wrong again. She rested her cheek against his shoulder and breathed deeply. He didn't smell of aftershave or even fabric conditioner. Leah wasn't entirely sure what she was breathing in except that judging by the effect it was having on her body, it had to contain a healthy dose of pheromones.

The song was far too short. Just as she'd closed her eyes and tried to imprint her brain with every sensation she was feeling so she could relive the happiness later, the music changed to something livelier. Duncan took her hand and lead her outside.

128

The flames from the hog roast had died down to a gentle glow. Leah couldn't see anyone else there, but then she wasn't really looking. All her senses were concentrated on Duncan.

"You look even more beautiful without your wellies," he said.

"Thanks, so do you. I mean..."

He laughed and pulled her into his arms, just as he'd done when they started dancing. This time she didn't rest her head on his shoulders, but lifted it up. He took the hint and kissed her.

His kiss was so gentle it barely registered on her lips, yet its effects could be felt rushing through her body. She wanted him to do it again. From the feel of him against her and the deep breaths he was taking, she guessed he felt the same way.

"So, you'll come out with me?"

It seemed more of a statement than a question, but she said 'yes' anyway.

Chapter 8

The next morning at breakfast, Leah again asked Jayne what was worrying her.

"It's probably nothing and I'm being silly getting myself in a state over it."

"I expect so, but what's nothing?"

"I've been bleeding a bit from, well my bottom. See why I wasn't keen to talk about it?" Jayne mumbled from behind her mug.

"I do, yes. Is that why you went to the doctor?"

Jayne nodded. "It's been uncomfortable for a while. Anyway, it might be nothing serious. I won't know until I have an examination. They want to stick cameras up my bum. That letter you asked about was a hospital appointment."

Leah put down her drink and spoke carefully. "You're going into hospital and you didn't tell me?"

"I'm not going."

"Oh yes you are!"

"I'm not. I only went to the doctor for some painkillers and he got in a flap and said he was referring me to a specialist. They only gave me a week's notice so I've cancelled it. That's why I had to go to the doctor the other day. He called me in and said I have to make another appointment as soon as possible."

"Then do it." If the specialist wanted to see Jayne that quickly, it would be because she potentially had a very serious condition requiring immediate action.

"How can I? I can't leave Rosemary to milk herself and the chickens to bring in their own eggs."

"No, but I could do it. How long will you be in?"

"For the examination just a few hours, I think. But treatment, if it's treatable, well that could mean I'm in for much longer."

"Oh, I see." Leah thought she could muddle through for a few days if needed and milk the cow and stop the other animals going hungry or short of water, but anything more than that was beyond her skill and strength.

Jayne was crying.

"Hey, come on," Leah said as she put her arm around Jayne's shoulders.

"I'm sorry, lovey. It's just... I can't even say it."

"I can't help if I don't know what's wrong."

"I don't think you can anyway. Oh, Leah it could be cancer. I have the symptoms of bowel cancer. What'll happen to the farm if I have?"

There was no answer she could give to that, so Leah just hugged her and let her cry. Leah hadn't cried much when she'd been accused of fraud and then discovered Adam didn't love her as much as she'd thought and doubted if it would have helped much if she had. What had helped her most was knowing she could count on Jayne for support and had somewhere to run away too. Jayne couldn't run away from her illness, but at least Leah could show some of the same kind of support Jayne had offered her.

"I'll do anything I can to help," she said.

"I know you will, lovey. Thank you." She blew her nose. "I suppose what I have to do is face up to this thing, make some kind of plan."

"Yes. I think the first stage is to go for that examination and see what we're up against. We can get as much done beforehand as possible and I'll look after this place while you're in. Do you think I could manage?"

"Yes, I'm sure you could, but what about work? It can't be much longer before they realise they were wrong about you and want you back again."

"I've heard nothing, so I don't think it'll be in the next couple of weeks, but even if it is, I'll help here. They'll owe me that much after what they've put me through. Actually, I'm due some leave anyway, tell you what, I'm going to call in and book a couple of days off, see how they handle that. Go ring your doctor and get an appointment."

"You're determined I'm going to it, aren't you?"

"I am. You're going. End of discussion."

Jayne smiled slightly. "So, that's the start of a plan then?"

Leah nodded and gave what she hoped was an encouraging grin.

"You know, calling work about taking time off is a good idea. They'll see you expect to be going back soon."

"Jayne, we're making a plan for you, not me."

"I know, I was just..."

"Trying to change the subject?"

"I suppose. Denial is quite appealing when you're scared. I never realised what a coward I was."

"Coward, you? You're one of the bravest people I know. I'm the coward. When I realised it wasn't working with Adam .. I started changing the subject! Now, you. You said it might be nothing serious?"

"Yes. A cyst the doctor said it could be. If it is, that's quite simple to sort out apparently. They just cauterise it and I rest for a few days and everything is fine." She gave a proper smile. "D'you know, I'm actually starting to think that's a possibility. How stupid will I feel if I've got myself into this state over a cyst?"

"A right lemon, I expect."

"Yeah. OK, I'll have that examination. Now you've bullied me into telling you about my problem you can jolly well cheer me up again. Spill the beans about what you and Duncan got up to at the party."

133

"I don't know what you can possibly mean," Leah said, trying to sound prim.

"Yes you do! I saw you dancing with him."

"Hmm, OK we did dance. Come to think of it, I saw you dancing with Jim, what did you two get up to?"

"Don't change the subject. Did he ask you out again?"

"Yes," Leah admitted. She felt her face flush as she remembered being in Duncan's arms and kissing him just before he asked.

"And did you say anything stupid?" Jayne demanded.

"What would count as stupid?"

"Anything other than 'yes'."

"In that case, no. I didn't say anything stupid."

"Good girl."

"So, what about you and Jim?"

"Oh, just dancing," Jayne said, but it was her turn to blush. "Come on, we've got chicken to feed."

Leah tried hard not to fantasise about what might happen on her date with Duncan. She wasn't sure how he felt about her; one kiss after a few glasses of wine didn't necessarily mean anything, however nice it was at the time.

Also she didn't know how long she was likely to

stay in Winkleigh Marsh. The idea of staying for a long time had become very appealing. She had got ahead of herself though. This was just a first date and she might be on the rebound. It would be best to see what happened before making any decisions.

"So, what are you wearing tonight?" Jayne asked.

"I hadn't really thought... well, that's not quite true. I haven't decided."

"Come on then, let's have a look at what you've got. That's if you don't mind? I don't mean to interfere."

"Of course not. It'll be fun. We're going for a meal in a pub, he said. The Frog and Bucket, do you know it?"

"Of it. Don't think I've been in there."

They went through the contents of Leah's wardrobe, giggling at the various possibilities. It was obvious Leah hadn't been thinking clearly when she came to Winkleigh Marsh. She hadn't packed anything suitable for mucking out the pigs, but that was simply because she didn't own anything like that. There were a few outfits almost suitable for walking in the countryside - provided of course it wasn't damp, or muddy, and the route avoided grass and hedges.

"How about this?" Jayne asked. She was holding up a slinky black silk top. "If you wore it with jeans it wouldn't be too dressy would it?"

"It's more undressy. I can't wear a bra with it and the front comes down to about here." She indicated a position that would expose plenty of cleavage.

"Sounds perfect."

"I'm not sure. I don't really know if this is just as friends or..."

"Wear that and I think you'll find out!"

Leah decided Jayne was right. She'd dress for a date and take her cue from him.

When Duncan arrived he was clutching a bunch of carnations. Duncan must have driven the four miles into town to get them which surely meant he'd given up his lunch hour for her.

Jayne took the flowers and said she'd put them in water.

"Thanks," Leah muttered. It was the first thing either she or Duncan had said since he'd arrived. Silly to be so nervous.

"Have a good time, both of you." Jayne turned Leah towards the door and gave Duncan a friendly shove.

"You look nice," Duncan said.

"Thanks, and thank you for the flowers."

"You're welcome."

She smiled up at him and suddenly they were both laughing. It seemed he'd felt as nervous as Leah had.

They chatted easily once they were in the car.

Duncan teased her, asking if he should expect a flood on the way to the restaurant.

"Why?"

"First time I met you involved mud, then it was rain. A flood seemed the next step."

"In that case, I'll try to arrange a dry disaster for you to rescue me from."

If it hadn't been for the illuminated sign outside showing a frog's crowned head sticking out the top of an old fashioned bucket, she'd have thought the pub was a farmhouse. When he pulled into the car park Duncan said, "It doesn't look much, but the food is great."

"Actually, I was just thinking it looked nice. No big electric signs for a chain or offering two for one deals."

"No, I don't think the turnover here would be high enough for them to be interested. Good job too - if I want microwaved food I'm quite capable of doing that myself."

Duncan was clearly well known in the pub and they were shown straight to a quiet table in the corner near, but not too near, a roaring log fire. Leah couldn't help wondering how many times he'd been there in the past and who with. She tried not to think about that.

They were handed menus. As Leah opened hers she spotted trout was listed. "Oooh, trout's my favourite fish."

"Have that then. It'll be really fresh as it's caught locally. A mate of mine supplies it."

"Sounds good." Far too late she realised she'd selected by far the most expensive item on the menu. Leah wondered what they'd do about the bill. She was used to Adam urging her to order the best dishes at trendy restaurants and always paying the bill, but Duncan probably wouldn't expect to pay for her meal. More likely they'd split the bill in half.

She scanned down for something cheaper. Other than baguettes, which didn't seem right as he had offered dinner, the next cheapest item was spaghetti Bolognese. Not one of her favourite dishes and the kind of thing she could get almost anywhere. "Or the spaghetti, I could have the spaghetti."

"No, you could have that anywhere. Have the local trout."

It had to be a good sign that they'd both thought the same thing at the same time. She made amends for her expensive food choice by drinking nothing more than a single diet coke.

Duncan asked about her life in London and her job. She didn't want to explain about the flat, which she'd bought and, until recently, shared with Adam. Mentioning Prophet Margin and the allegations against her was no more appealing, but he made sympathetic queries about her troubles. She found herself blurting out about the horror of her boss believing the charges could be possible and about Adam not backing her up.

"Sounds like you're well rid of him. I take it you are rid of him?"

"Oh, yes." But was that true? Getting him to buy her out of the flat might be messy and would take time and she'd have to go back to work at Prophet Margin. "Well, getting that way."

"Oh, right."

"Gosh, listen to me rambling on about my problems and ranting about my ex boyfriend. That's not what a man wants to hear on a first date." Leah blushed. "I didn't mean there would be more. I, oh dear."

Duncan reached across the table to take her hand. "It's all right. I think what you need is a friend, so friends for now?"

"Yes. Thank you."

"Now, what about dessert?"

It didn't take much to persuade her that the Frog and Bucket's treacle tart was not to be missed.

Duncan did kiss her goodbye after driving her home, but it wasn't quite the same kind of kiss as at the party. Although slightly disappointed by that she did think he was right about her needing a friend. She shouldn't jump straight into another relationship, no matter how tempting that might be, while her life was so unsettled. It wouldn't be fair to either of them.

Sadly, by the time things with work were sorted out, she'd be headed back to London and wouldn't see Duncan again.

That thought wasn't appealing and wasn't accurate. She'd be back down to Winkleigh Marsh whenever she could and she'd find ways to see Duncan and, if he wanted to, he could find ways to see her.

When Leah got back to Primrose Cottage, Jayne had already gone to bed. Tarragon was still awake and he greeted her enthusiastically. That was one of the things she loved about living there, someone was always pleased to see her, even if he did have four legs and a waggy tail. Perhaps that was one of the reasons Jayne had got herself a dog. It must be lonely living there alone since her parents had died, one just a month after the other. Leah remembered the red rose left on the doorstep on Valentine's Day. She hoped Jim had sent it.

The following morning, Leah noticed Rosemary acting strangely. She seemed distressed and at one point it looked as though she intended to attack her own two year old daughter, Rosepetal. Leah had no idea what the symptoms of mad cow disease were, but worried maybe that was what it looked like. Although she didn't want to bring Jayne bad news, it must be better to act quickly in the hope that something could be done. She ran in to Primrose Cottage.

"Whatever's the matter, lovey?"

"It's Rosemary, I think she's... well, I don't know what to think."

Jayne followed her back into the yard. They arrived just in time to see Rosemary lunge at Rosepetal.

"Oh good, she's bulling," Jayne said.

"This is good?"

"Yes, she's ready to get in calf again. That jumping onto Rosepetal is one of the signs, it's just an instinctive hormonal thing. Sorry you were worried."

"That's OK." She giggled. "And there was me thinking I knew something about the facts of life!"

"You've got a lot to learn, my girl."

"Maybe. You said this was good, so does that mean you want her to have another calf?"

Jayne nodded.

"OK, so where will you get a bull from? You'll need one of those, even I know that much."

"Actually, no. I'll have her artificially inseminated. Don't look like that, it's not as icky as it sounds."

"Why don't you use a bull?"

"Keeping one myself wouldn't be worth it for two cows. By buying the semen I can choose from a vast selection of bulls who're known to produce good calves without difficult births, or to meet whatever other criteria I might have."

"You make it sound like you pick them from a

catalogue."

"Yes, I do. Only works for bulls though, men are an entirely different matter! I'll call Home Farm; if they're having any cows done in the next day or two, I'll take Rosemary over there, just like I did with Rosepetal, or if I'm lucky G-B will arrange transportation. As I told you, he's not all bad."

"That does seem quite helpful," Leah conceded.

After she'd made her call, Jayne explained it was good news. "For me and two of my girls. The AI man is visiting Home Farm tomorrow and Duncan will collect Rosemary."

"Oh, that's good," Leah said, trying to look as though she was pleased on Rosemary's behalf as much as her own.

"It is. I reckon I might get a lie-in. That's if you think you can handle the milking and helping load Rosemary in the trailer?"

Leah saw how tired Jayne looked and quickly agreed.

"Of course." It would be a good test for when Jayne went into hospital.

It'd also make a nice change for Duncan to see her being competent at managing a cow. She didn't allow herself to analyse why she was so keen for him to see she fitted well into the country way of life when she'd be returning to her job in London soon.

Leah finished milking Rosemary and let in the young calves for their share. She'd milked Rosemary for as long as she could manage and used every ounce of strength in her arms. She couldn't even face re-buttoning her top. She'd noticed she'd done it up wrong whilst milking. If she'd had a plan to impress Duncan then that small detail wasn't going to be the thing that ruined the good impression. Leah knew she looked tired.

Getting up early hadn't been easy, partly because she'd had trouble sleeping. She thought about Duncan as she'd tossed and turned, but he wasn't the only thing on her mind. Worry about Jayne and the current and future responsibilities of looking after the farm animals had concerned her too.

Leah giggled. How long had it been since the monthly figures and an upcoming powerpoint presentation or dinner party had been what kept her awake at night? She hadn't missed her old life as much as she'd expected.

Tarragon wagged his tail and gave a welcoming yap when a vehicle pulled into the yard.

"Morning, Jayne," Duncan called. "Is Rosemary ready for her date?" His attention was on the dog as he approached the shed where Rosemary and Leah were waiting.

"I'm just fixing her mascara," Leah called.

Damn, why had she said that? She'd not had time to put any on that morning, or brush her hair. It might have been better not to draw his attention to the subject of making the best of one's appearance. She had brushed her teeth at least. She couldn't face going out before she'd done that. Her best plan was probably to get so close he couldn't focus on her dishevelled appearance and instead got a whiff of her fresh minty breath. The idea was quite appealing, but she reminded herself it was her competence she was trying to impress with.

"Leah?"

"Yes. I'm head milkmaid today."

"Is Jayne OK?"

He sounded so concerned Leah wondered if he'd guessed she was ill.

"Don't worry, she's just having a lie-in."

"Do her good, I expect."

"Yes. What happens next?"

"Next? Well I hadn't really thought, maybe we could go for a drink on Saturday?"

"Rosemary doesn't drink."

"What? Oh, right. We get her in the trailer and I take her over to Home Farm." He undid the ramp on the back of the trailer as he spoke. "The AI man does the business and I bring her back. I'm afraid I can't say what time that'll be, but I promise we'll take care of her and she'll be home in time for milking. I assure you, my intentions with regards her are entirely honourable."

"You make it sound simple."

"It is, I know Rosemary. She's a pushover." Duncan jumped into the back of the trailer, reappearing almost immediately with a bucket. He rattled it towards the cow. "Come on girl, a nice bucket of sugarbeet for you." He let the cow stick her head in the bucket and lick up a few of the dark pellets, then backed away from her towards the trailer. She followed him out the barn and up into the trailer. Duncan closed the ramp behind her.

"Do you have time for a cup of tea or anything?"

"No, sorry. I've got to get back and sort out the rest of the cows who're competing with Rosemary for the AI man's attention. Don't worry, it'll all be over soon and she'll be back without even knowing what's happened."

"Seems a bit of a shame for poor old Rosemary."

"Why?"

"Not exactly romantic, is it?"

"I'll play her soft music if it'll make you feel better."

She grinned. OK, he was teasing, but he did understand what she meant.

Leah had sorted out the milk, fed Rosepetal and thrown more logs onto the Aga before she heard Jayne moving around upstairs. She switched on the kettle and got out the items required for breakfast, to give the illusion she had everything under control.

145

Luckily the fire hadn't gone out completely and the logs that had dried on the hearth all evening soon caught.

The tea was made and bacon sizzling in a pan when Jayne came into the kitchen. Leah grinned as it occurred to her the scene was almost the exact opposite of her first morning at Primrose Cottage. OK, she hadn't found it easy to get up in time to milk Rosemary and her arms were aching a little from the effort, but she'd coped.

"Goodness, I can't believe it's so late. I don't think I've slept for so long since I was a teenager," Jayne said.

"I expect you needed it. I didn't like to say, but you have been looking a bit tired lately."

"Feeling it too, to be honest. Now, how about you?"

"I slept for about three minutes. Rosemary has been milked and collected though. Sorry, I haven't done anything else. I went back to sleep after the alarm went off and got up in a panic."

Leah served up breakfast.

"Thanks, love. This is a real treat."

"So, you think I'll be OK to look after things while you're in hospital?"

"Well, yes, ordinarily I think you would. There's just one thing that you won't be prepared for."

"What's that? There's time for me to learn, so

whatever it is, it's not getting you out of going to hospital."

"I didn't mean it that way. I'd been so far in denial about going into hospital that it hadn't occurred to me the timing would be a problem. Rosepetal is due to calve."

"Oh. OK, not time for me to learn. What happens? Presumably you don't actually check her into a maternity ward at the vet's and have her fill in a questionnaire about epidurals and birthing pools?"

Jayne laughed. "No. Chances are, she'll have it fine by herself, but if she doesn't the vet will come out."

"How will he know to come?"

"You call if there's a problem."

"Ah but I won't have a clue if there's a problem. Can't I just call the vet as soon as anything happens, or is that not allowed?"

"You could, but you can't keep calling. It'll cost and it's not fair. You can't expect the vet to sit with her all night waiting for something to happen."

"No, I suppose not." Leah knew she'd panic the moment Rosepetal even breathed slightly more heavily than usual, but didn't want Jayne to postpone her hospital appointment yet again. Besides, she wanted to prove to herself, and anyone else who might be interested, that she could handle life on a farm.

"Maybe we can arrange for you to see a calf being

born? Do you think that'd help?"

"Maybe." Leah wasn't convinced it would help enough for her to be of any real help.

"We'll ask Duncan. There are plenty of in-calf cows at Home Farm."

"That would be very useful." Any experience and training she got were bound to be an improvement on her current state of ignorance.

When Duncan came back with Rosemary, Jayne invited him in for tea and explained about Rosepetal's imminent motherhood.

Duncan just nodded. Cows having calves didn't seem like big news to him.

"I might not be here when it happens," Jayne said.

That got his attention all right. He understood that if Leah was to be the attending midwife, there was more to the story.

Leah said, "I, we, think it would be good if I could see a cow giving birth before Rosepetal has her calf. Help prepare me a bit."

"Yes, I see. We have plenty of cows due to calve over the next few weeks. I'll give you a call when it looks like a good time to come and watch."

"Thank you," Leah and Jayne said together.

The three of them got through two pots of tea and most of a walnut cake before Duncan said he'd better get going. "Leah, before I go, come out and see that Rosemary is OK. I wouldn't want you thinking I'd been unkind to the old dear."

Jayne seemed to suddenly choke on a piece of cake. Either that or she was smothering a laugh.

Rosemary looked perfectly content lying on her straw bed and chewing the cud.

"Looks like she had a good time," Leah admitted.

"So that drink we mentioned, how about it?" Duncan asked.

"Yes, I'd like that. Thanks."

"Pick you up about seven on Saturday, then?"

He gently brushed her lips with his own before leaving.

Chapter 9

Leah learned as much as she could from Jayne about looking after the animals. When she wasn't worrying about all the things that could go wrong whilst Jayne was in hospital, she worried about all the things that could go wrong on her date with Duncan.

He'd offered friendship. Was that all he wanted? He did seem to want quite an affectionate type of friendship which included a few kisses and she was happy to encourage that. She'd need to be subtle though, she might make it too obvious she fancied him and scare him off. That would be a disaster.

Leah wanted to get to know him better, a lot better, but she also needed his help in learning about calving. Not only that but he seemed the only person who was making any attempt to get Mr Gilmore-Bunce to honour his obligations as a landlord.

Leah confessed some of her worries to Jayne as she waited for Duncan to collect her. "I don't know what we'll talk about."

"Rubbish, you've found plenty to talk about up to now, haven't you?"

"Yes, but we don't really have anything in common."

"Then talk about your differences! Honestly, it sounds as though you're trying to make things difficult."

"I'm not. It's just... well, I don't exactly want to remind him of our differences and that I'm not the obvious choice to fit into a farmer's life." Leah felt herself blush.

"Oh, I see." She gave a smile that anyone less charitable than Leah would have described as a smirk. "You could swap stories about the disgraceful things you got up to as children. That should break the ice."

"Maybe he didn't get up to anything disgraceful?"

"Oh yes he did!"

"You sound very sure."

"Of course I am. Just like with you when you were here it was often me who was the victim of his pranks."

"You were? But I thought he was new here?"

"Oh! Yes. He used to come here as a child. Well not here here, but to this area."

Tarragon yapped and bounded to the door.

"Looks like he's here."

"Yes. But Jayne, you said..."

Jayne wasn't listening, she'd gone to open the door to Duncan. She let Tarragon out, then scolded him for bounding out to greet Duncan. "Daft animal, get back here, you'll trip him up. Don't get him all muddy."

Leah frowned at the fuss she was making. Tarragon never jumped up at people and Duncan was casually dressed.

"Hello, Jayne," Duncan said. "Are you OK?"

It was nice of him to be concerned, but he seemed more interested in greeting Jayne than looking at her. Why hadn't either of them said they'd known each other before? Was there something else they weren't telling her?

"Duncan, I was just telling Leah how we've actually known each other since we were kids," Jayne said.

Of course, as Duncan wasn't all that much younger than Jayne, they'd have been children at the same time.

"Oh good. Leah, I did want to tell you the truth, but we thought..."

"It's my fault," Jayne interrupted. "Leah, you were so set against G-B that when I realised who your dishy tractor driver was, I didn't like to say."

Leah blushed when Jayne described Duncan as dishy, he was bound to guess it was Leah who'd told her that.

"But it's best you know the truth," Duncan said.

"Absolutely and anyway, you don't hate G-B anymore, do you?" Jayne asked.

"No, I suppose not." She was ashamed of her previous irrational dislike of a man she'd never met, especially as two people she really liked both had a different opinion. Her beliefs that he'd deliberately got her into trouble at work and he'd neglected Primrose Cottage were both wrong, but she hadn't been mistaken about the abrupt communications she'd received from him demanding immediate changes to his investments or sudden withdrawals all without any kind of explanation or thanks. "I still think he's rude, pompous and arrogant, but I admit I over-reacted a bit."

Duncan looked uncomfortable.

"Right, but you wouldn't blame anyone else for his actions?" Jayne asked.

"No."

"Duncan is a relation. He used to visit Home Farm in the school holidays."

"Oh! It's surprising we never bumped into each other."

"Actually, I think we may have done," Duncan said. "I do remember a little girl with hair the colour of yours running away from some Llamas."

"Yes, that would have been me. It was all Jayne's fault."

Duncan grinned. "I believe you. Come on, I'll buy you a drink and you can tell me all about it."

Conversation was easy after that. Leah told him

153

about all her visits to Primrose Cottage and her obsession with the orphan lambs. Duncan tried to remember where he'd have been at the time and to work out if they'd ever met then.

"Probably not. I went to boarding school so my parents were keen to keep me with them during the holidays. About the only times I left my grandparent's smallholding was when I walked across Home Farm fields to spend my pocket money in the village shop. Now that's odd - I took the same route as the day you had to rescue me, but I never got chased by cows. I don't remember there being any, it was more like walking through a maze."

"That's exactly what it would have been; a field of maize."

Leah didn't know what maize was, or how Duncan could have known and remembered what had been growing there.

"It's like sweetcorn, used to make silage. I used to ride in the tractor sometimes when it was sown and every year, we all picked some and cooked it in its husks on portable barbecues at the side of the field. The type grown for animal feed isn't reckoned to be as good as that grown as a vegetable, but picked young and eaten straight away, it's delicious."

"I remember Jayne telling me about that. Well, taunting rather than telling because I love sweetcorn and was always back at school before that happened. She was really mean to me sometimes." Leah gave

154

what she hoped was a cute looking pout.

"She was a bad girl all round as I remember." Duncan told her about the occasion he'd caught Jayne and a boyfriend in the hay loft at Home Farm. "I didn't actually see anything other than the two of them sneaking out, but she went so red when I mentioned it, I knew she'd been up to something she shouldn't."

Leah giggled. Twenty years afterwards didn't seem too long for her to continue the teasing on the subject.

"To be honest, I was so young and innocent I thought they might have been drinking cider."

Leah wouldn't mind giving him a practical lesson in what a couple of teenagers were likely to have been getting up to in a hay loft. Good thing he wasn't really the mind reader she'd thought him the first time she met him.

"Maybe they were?" she asked. She didn't want to give the impression she had a one track mind.

"Trust me, they weren't! I suspect my turning up just then blighted her love life for months."

"I don't think either of us helped her love life much. I pulled a mean trick with some frogs one night when her parents went out and left her baby-sitting me."

In the pub, they sat opposite each other, both of them leaning over the table. There was plenty of eye contact and some of the physical kind too. Their hands occasionally brushed as they reached for their drinks and sometimes they touched deliberately. It was just a playful slap of his arm when he was cheeky or touch of her hand when making a point, but it felt good.

Talking to Duncan about their almost shared childhood made her feel much closer to him. When he held her hand to walk with her to his car, it felt perfectly natural. They didn't talk so much on the drive home, but it felt friendly and companionable, not awkward. Leah had to concentrate hard not to stare at him all the way home.

She wasn't surprised when his kiss goodnight was more than a brief peck. He held her close and moved slowly, giving plenty of time for her to offer a cheek if she didn't want to be kissed on the lips. She didn't turn her face away.

Duncan didn't release her immediately after the kiss. He held her gently and said he hoped to see her again soon.

"I'd like that." She was aware of the blood rushing round her body and felt warm and happy.

"We're busy with the first calves at the moment. Hopefully I'll be able to get you over to see a birth soon, but I'll give you a call soon anyway."

"Great, I look forward to it."

She was a little disappointed he hadn't arranged

another date immediately, but she tried not to show it. He was definitely being more than just friendly. That would have to do for now.

Duncan phoned quite early Sunday morning. "It looks as though we're going to get some calves today. You're very welcome to come over, but I'm not sure if I'll be able to come and get you."

"That's OK, I'll drive round once we've finished here. I won't miss everything if I don't get there straight away?"

"No. Once one calves, it's quite common for that to set the others off, but the first one has only just started."

"OK, I'll get there as soon as I can."

Jayne overheard the conversation and, guessing what it was about, said, "Best go now. You'll want to see the first signs of calving, so you know what to look out for."

"Yes, that's true." And it gave her the opportunity to spend more time with Duncan. "Thanks, Jayne, I'll see you later."

Leah saw Duncan's car in the yard at Home Farm and parked next to it. Beeping her horn seemed rude and she didn't want to go to the farmhouse and risk coming across Mr Gilmore-Bunce, so she followed the sound of cows mooing in the hope of finding Duncan.

She spotted him the other side of a huge pen, full of enormous cows. They seemed even more massive than the ones who'd scared her the day she got stuck in the mud. Duncan didn't seem bothered though. He was in with them, shaking straw about for their bedding.

He saw her and waved. "Come here, you'll want to see this."

Leah would much rather see whatever it was from a safe distance, but it was clear he expected her to join him.

"It better be worth it," she muttered under her breath, before climbing onto the metal bars of the pen. She swung her leg over the top and took several steps without incident. The cows nearest her were lying down. She negotiated safely round them, then found her way blocked by a standing cow. The thing was so tall she couldn't see over it to where Duncan was waiting.

After a moment's panic, Leah saw it was chewing the cud. That placid behaviour reminded her of Rosemary and made her braver. She put her hand on the animal's back and gently pushed, just as Jayne had shown her to do when she needed to move one of the Jerseys.

"Move over, girl," she whispered.

The cow obeyed and wandered slowly out of Leah's way. Gosh, she was getting to be a proper farm hand. With considerably more confidence, Leah walked ever closer to Duncan. Soon another cow blocked her progress. This one's belly was huge, it had to be having triplets at least.

Leah decided there was just room for her to squeeze by.

As Leah edged alongside the big beast, another cow had the same idea and came towards her. That one was the fattest yet. The one at her side had nowhere to go, the one approaching didn't have space to move aside and a glance behind her showed Leah she was being followed, so couldn't make a hasty retreat. Couldn't the cow coming towards her see it was going to crush her, or didn't it care?

She put her hand out like a policeman stopping traffic and ordered it to, "Stay."

The cow kept coming.

Leah's throat became so tight, she wasn't able to repeat her command, let alone yell to Duncan for help. She closed her eyes and waited.

The smell of cow was really strong and Leah could feel their warmth. Then came the impact. First it was like being jostled on the underground. Then nothing. She opened her eyes. The cow had gone. Did that mean she was dead and it had walked right through her?

"She's not due until next week," Duncan said.

Leah realised she was holding onto a cow for support. She tried taking a step. Everything seemed to be in working order and although Duncan was giving her an odd look, it wasn't one that suggested he was conversing with the dead.

"You OK?"

"I thought I was going to get squished."

Duncan grinned. "Never looks like there's room for them to get by, does it? Luckily their big bellies just swing out the way."

"I'm glad my near death experience amused you!"

"Oh, Leah! I'd forgotten this was all new to you. I'm sorry if you were worried, but honestly I wouldn't have got you to come in here if there was any danger."

She took a few deep breaths. "So, what did you want me to see?"

As Duncan pointed out cows in various stages of pregnancy and explained how she could tell, she forgot her annoyance. He was trying to help her and he had contacted her at the first opportunity and invited her over, so she should be grateful.

"Those two there, which will calve first?" He pointed out two cows side be side with their backs to them.

"That one. It looks like it's producing milk."

"Quite right. With Rosepetal, because it's her first calf, the difference will be even more obvious."

"I'll keep a close eye on her. Jayne says that when a cow is about to start calving you can tell. Is that right?"

"Yes. It's difficult to explain, but once you know the cow, you know when something's happening."

"That's why you knew there'd be calves today."

He nodded. "Yes. although knowing the date they got in calf is obviously a big help too."

"Is it some of these?"

"No, we've already separated out the ones we expected to calve today."

"To give them some privacy?"

He grinned again. "You can think of it that way if you like, but really it's for safety. As you've seen, there's not a lot of room in here. We bring them all together like this when they're due so we can monitor them regularly. They've just been here a couple of days and we'll be taking more out each day over the next few weeks."

"A busy time?"

"Very. We try to get them calving in two batches. One now and one lot had theirs about three months ago and are just getting in calf again now."

"Like Rosemary. I see."

"Remember I said that when one cow starts to give birth it sets the others off?"

"Yes."

"That's happened here. A cow who wasn't due for a couple of days seems to be starting early."

"Will she be OK?"

"Fine, but I want to get her into a separate pen. Give me a hand?"

"OK. Which one is she?"

"You tell me."

Leah looked round the pen. Every cow had a different pattern of black and white markings, but to her they all looked very similar. She couldn't even recognise the two she thought were going to crush her. No, actually she could. The fidgety one in the corner looked as though it was the one which pushed past her. It might have felt it had an urgent need to be somewhere, but it didn't seem to know what to do with itself now it was there.

She looked at each of the other cows in turn. They weren't doing a lot. A couple had their heads in the trough which ran along one end of the pen and were eating what looked like particularly horrendous muesli. One was drinking from the water tank. The rest were all lying or standing while they chewed. Her attention kept being drawn back to the fidgeter. That cow was the only one not chewing and it kept turning round as though checking no one were sneaking up on her. It seemed odd for a cow to be paranoid.

"Oh! It's her, isn't it? The fidgety one?" Leah pointed.

Duncan grinned. "Yep and luckily she's got herself

right by the gate, so getting her out will be easy."

It was. Duncan opened the gate to let her out and the cow, prompted by a few nudges from Leah, followed him into a separate stall. They shut her in and went to check on the rest of the cows. None had actually started to give birth, but Leah believed him when Duncan said it wouldn't be long. Unless it was her imagination, they did seem as though they were expecting something to happen.

"Let's have a cup of tea and come back later," Duncan suggested.

"Good plan."

He set off for the farmhouse.

"You won't get into trouble will you?" Leah said.

"Trouble, why?"

"For taking me inside and..."

"No, silly."

Duncan had a key to the house and clearly felt at home there. She'd forgotten he was related to that awful Gilmore-Bunce, who luckily wasn't at home. Of course hc wasn't; there was work to do.

The house was large with lots of furniture, but that didn't stop Duncan from sitting close to her on a leather sofa. It felt good to be with him like that; a mixture of excitement and relaxation. She was pleased she was learning from him and had been able to help him move the cow. Hopefully he too had noticed they made a good team.

163

By the time they'd drunk the tea and returned to the maternity stalls, a cow had gone into labour. Leah watched fascinated as the cow huffed and puffed, looking just like a woman having contractions, except it was standing and fairly quiet. She almost didn't notice Duncan put his arm around her shoulders as he watched with her.

After a while the cow lay down. That didn't seem to suit her though as she thrashed about a bit as though trying to find a comfortable position. She soon stood up again. Behind her was a calf covered in slime.

"She's had it!"

He gave her shoulders a quick squeeze. "Yes. Don't be worried if Rosepetal takes much longer though. This is the fifth calf for this one. First calves often take hours."

Leah nodded. She was feeling a lot happier about her role as temporary midwife.

"She did it all on her own. Jayne said they do, but I couldn't imagine it."

The new mother began energetically licking her calf. Within just a few minutes, it had got shakily to its feet and started to drink.

"I feel all emotional."

Duncan ruffled her hair. "Want to see it again?"

"She's having twins?" It didn't seem possible. The cow was huge, but so was the calf.

"Nope. Come on." He grabbed her hand.

They went to look at fidgety. She hadn't started to calve, but the cow in the stall next to her had. The second cow lay down for the whole process and took a bit longer, but everything went just as smoothly. By the time the second calf was on its feet and drinking, the fidgety cow was laid down making the heaving movements with her belly which meant another calf was on its way. After half an hour, Duncan suggested another cup of tea.

"Should we leave her?"

"She'll be fine for a while."

They didn't take so long drinking the second cup of tea, but Duncan sat just as close. He only talked about cows and gave advice on what to do when Rosepetal calved, but with him sitting so close she could feel his breath on her cheek, the conversation seemed very intimate.

Two hours after Leah had first realised the cow was about to calve, two feet appeared from the Friesian's back end.

"There it is!" Leah cried.

"Yes, she's doing fine."

After a few more heaves, they could see the calf's nose.

"That's a really good sign. Means the calf is the right way round. If you can see back legs, or there's

165

no head it's likely to be a difficult birth."

Although Duncan kept assuring Leah everything was fine, with words and hugs, the cow continued to heave without making any more progress.

"Shouldn't you call a vet?"

"There's no need, but she's been at it a while; we'd better give her a hand."

"We?"

"You wanted some training."

Leah could only nod. If she chickened out now how could she hope to help Rosepetal or earn Duncan's respect?

Duncan opened the door to the stall and stepped inside. He waited a moment then indicated Leah should join him.

"Do everything slowly and gradually, we don't want to alarm her."

No need; Leah was alarmed enough for the both of them.

Slowly they approached the cow and knelt behind her.

"Easy there, Wanda," Duncan said as he put his hand on the cow's back.

"Wanda?" Leah asked.

"You didn't think Rosemary and Rosepetal were the only cows with names?"

As that's exactly what she had thought, Leah kept

quiet.

"What we're going to do is help the calf out, by gently pulling each time she pushes. Don't jerk and don't use too much force."

"Right."

She must have sounded as scared as she felt, because Duncan squeezed her hand.

"I'll tell you exactly when."

He helped her get hold of the calf's ankles, then knelt behind her. He reached round and put his hands just above hers. Once she was in his arms, she didn't feel so worried.

The cow heaved.

"Now, gently."

Leah hardly dared pull at all, but she guessed Duncan was using more strength.

"OK, stop."

She released her grip.

"Keep hold, just don't pull again until I say."

"Sorry."

"You're doing fine."

She felt fine, maybe because she could feel the heat of his body, pressed against her.

"OK, pull now."

They pulled and for a second it seemed the calf's head would come free, then it disappeared back inside its mother.

"I think the head will come next time."

It did and a few pulls later, the rest followed. Duncan quickly lifted its leg, dropped it back down and said, "Let's go."

By the time they'd got themselves out and shut the door, Wanda was on her feet, licking the calf.

Tears coursed down Leah's cheeks.

"You were right about the emotional bit," Duncan said. He held her close and kissed her forehead.

"Don't you feel at all emotional at a birth?"

"I'm pleased they're both fine and that it's a heifer calf. Wanda's a good milker, so her new calf will eventually join the herd." He led her to a tap in the yard where they washed their hands.

"You'll have to think of a name for her then."

"It'll be Wanda."

"Wanda the second?"

"About the hundred and second. Each cow is named after its mother, so she's got sisters and aunts also called Wanda."

"What's the point of that?"

"It helps with identification. They all have official ear tag numbers by law, but you can't remember who's related to who so they have a name and number too. This Wanda is Wanda six-one meaning she's Wanda the sixth's first calf, or at least the first female we've kept."

"That's boring. I'm going to give Rosepetal's calf a nice name."

"You do that."

She thought for a minute she'd offended him, but he grinned at her.

"So, now you're all trained up, perhaps you'll let me take you somewhere to celebrate?"

"Don't you have to stay with the cows until they've all calved?"

"Not every night. Phil and Jake take regular turns too, plus there are a couple of others who do a shift when they're needed."

Of course, Home Farm was a much bigger place than Jayne's smallholding, one person couldn't be expected to do everything. "I've never seen anyone else about on the farm."

"No." He looked slightly embarrassed. "I've kept them out the way."

"What's wrong with them?"

"Nothing. Well, nothing except them both being single and younger than me and..." He shrugged. "So, will you agree to come out with me again? Say yes quick before you get a look at the competition."

He said it as though he were joking, but Leah had the impression he really didn't want her to prefer the elusive Phil or Jake over himself. She wanted to show him he had nothing to worry about.

"Yes, but it should be my treat, to thank you."

"There's no need for that."

"Yes there is. Thank you so much for today, it's been amazing." She kissed his cheek.

"You want to thank me, you can give me a proper kiss."

"Oh, could I?" She tried to look as though she were thinking about it rather than fighting the urge to give him the most passionate kiss he'd ever experienced.

"Either that, or you can come with me and I'll show you what us country types get up to in hay barns."

Regretfully she decided a kiss was all he was going to get. She took a step toward him and slid her arms around his neck. As he pulled her close and lowered his lips to hers, she felt a jolt of pleasure surge through her. If that's what it was like to have him kiss her, what would it be like if they...

Her legs felt a little shaky as he held her hand and walked her back to the car, but that was probably just from the excitement of seeing three cows give birth. Or maybe not.

Chapter 10

Leah and Jayne spent a busy day giving the animals extra bedding and moving foodstuffs nearer those which weren't fed in the yard, so Leah wouldn't have too much to do while Jayne was in hospital. Leah was glad of the work as it helped stop her think about two disturbing pieces of post she'd received.

The first one she opened was from the professional organisation she belonged to. It was long and boring, explaining her rights and the action that could be taken on her behalf if she so wished. Leah couldn't get interested. She wanted her name cleared, of course, but only because no one would want to live under allegations of embezzlement, not because she really wanted to return to her old life. Maybe she'd feel differently once everything was cleared up.

The second item was a small package addressed in Adam's handwriting. She supposed it would be legal papers concerning the flat, maybe bills he expected her to contribute towards. Instead the brown paper covered a copy of John Steinbeck's 'Of Mice and Men.' She'd told him she'd read and enjoyed it at school and he must have seen it in a bookshop and remembered.

There was a short note, saying just, 'As the saying goes, I saw this and thought of you. Adam.' There was a short diagonal stroke after his name as though he'd started to draw a kiss and stopped halfway through - or perhaps had just made an accidental mark on the paper.

Leah opened the book and gasped. Inside was a stamp from her old school. Flipping through she saw pencilled notes in the margin. They weren't hers, but she had done exactly the same thing in her own copy. Sending it to her was nice, if surprising, thing for him to do. She couldn't help wondering if there was any motive behind it.

She'd shown both the letter and the book to Jayne. "Looks like you'll be OK financially," she said after scanning the letter. "At least, I think that's what it means."

Leah confirmed it did and they both looked at the book. Leah explained its significance.

"Would it have been expensive?" Jayne asked.

"Probably cost less than the postage. Do you think he was just being nice?"

"You know him better than me, but presumably he's capable of being nice. You wouldn't have moved in with him otherwise."

"True."

"Talking of nice, the pigs are hungry."

There wasn't much time for thinking after that.

As they came in for their supper, Leah's mobile rang.

"Hi, Duncan," she said.

Jayne grinned and disappeared into the kitchen.

"I was hoping I could tempt you to come out with me again?"

"Yes, I'd like to... sometime," she said wondering when she could say she'd be free.

"No pressure. I thought we could go to the pub tomorrow night. There's a quiz on and me and my mates usually make up a team, but if you don't fancy it..."

Obviously she hadn't sounded very enthusiastic.

"It's just that Jayne's going into hospital the day after tomorrow."

"Oh yes, of course. I'm sorry, it hadn't occurred to me that you wouldn't want to leave the farm. I understand though."

"That's OK. Shall I ring you when I'm free?"

Or you could come round here, she could have said if she'd had the nerve.

"Yeah, sure. Give Jayne my best."

"I will. Speak to you soon."

Jayne put her head round the door frame and asked for an explanation.

"He suggested the pub tomorrow night, but..."

173

"That doesn't sound like you said yes."

"No. I didn't think I should."

"Why on earth not?"

Leah didn't like to explain. Jayne had spent most of the last week apologising for being a nuisance and burdening Leah with the work of the farm. She couldn't let Jayne think she was also spoiling a beautiful romance.

"Oh, you know. I don't want to rush into anything."

"Leah, is this because of me going in for those stupid tests?"

Luckily for Leah, Jayne's house phone rang, saving her from having to respond.

"Jim, nice to hear from you," Jayne said.

There was a pause.

"Jim Applemore, I'm having a test, not dying!"

Another pause.

"But you haven't asked me out in years."

Too late, because it had become too interesting to leave, Leah realised she hadn't been as tactful as Jayne and left the room during the phone call.

After quite a long pause, Jayne said, "Silly girl said no."

Guessing she was the silly girl, Leah gestured frantically at Jayne, trying to signal that she wanted to say something and Jayne should say she'd call Jim back.

"Hang on, Jim. She's having some kind of fit, can I call you back?"

"The silly girl said no?" Leah demanded as soon as Jayne hung up.

"Yes."

"Why didn't you say yes?"

Jayne raised her eyebrows in an exaggerated fashion. "Me?"

"Yes, Jim asked you out, didn't he?"

"Yes."

"And you said no. Why?"

"Well..."

"Don't want to rush into anything?"

"Exactly. Oh." Jayne's face showed she remembered Leah using that excuse just minutes before and that she'd not accepted it.

"You like him, he likes you. Where did he want to take you?"

"To dinner at the Frog and Bucket tomorrow night," Jayne admitted.

"It's nice there. Say yes. Unless... he's not involved with anyone else, is he?"

"No."

"So, say yes. Honestly, I can't see why you two didn't get together years ago."

Jayne frowned then her face brightened as though she'd had a brilliant idea. "I can't say yes. You turned down Duncan to stay in with me, so it would be very rude of me to go out."

Leah held up her phone. "I'll say yes if you will."

Jayne picked up the receiver.

Leah flipped open her mobile.

Jayne punched a button on her phone.

Leah followed suit. It felt like they were lining up for a duel.

Jayne stabbed her finger at another button.

Leah selected Duncan's number.

By the time they'd both contacted their prospective dates, the women were giggling at each other. Fortunately neither man took offence at that, nor minded the sudden changes of heart.

Jayne was so nervous the day before her hospital visit, both about her examination and leaving Leah in charge of the farm, that Leah was relieved not to be spending the evening with her. She felt sure she'd say the wrong thing and upset her. Jim, she was sure, would distract Jayne from her worries.

Leah was excited about the idea of meeting some of Duncan's friends. That suggested he perhaps wanted her included in his world, rather than to just pass briefly through it and soon be forgotten. She decided to make herself memorable and wore her new pink, low cut top and figure hugging jeans.

Jayne clearly approved of her choice and when Jim arrived, he made it clear he did too.

"Oh stop it! You're chatting up the wrong woman," she told him.

"Just trying to make her jealous," he stage whispered, before taking Jayne away.

Duncan arrived almost immediately afterwards.

He kissed her cheek, then said, "Nice top, very... pink." That gave him the excuse for a long, lingering look.

"In a good way?"

"Definitely." He kissed her again to make his point. Thankfully he seemed to have forgotten his suggestion of them being friends. She didn't need a friend - she had Jayne for that.

The pub was full, or more accurately, over full. Quiz nights were obviously as popular here as in London.

"No team have won for weeks, so we've had lots of rollovers and there's a big prize at stake," Duncan explained as he led her to a table which already had three men sat around it.

He introduced Leah to his friends. "This sorry looking bunch are Phil, Smudge and Jake." He pointed to each in turn. All three were in their mid twenties, attractive and looked fit and strong. With Duncan, Phil and Jake at Home Farm, it was a wonder there wasn't a constant stream of single

177

women wandering about getting stuck in mud or otherwise needing attention. Actually, for all she knew, there might be.

"Lads, this is Leah," Duncan said.

The three men nodded and grinned at her as though they'd worked that out already and had heard something amusing about her. Who'd been saying what?

"Hi, Leah. Where's Duncan been keeping you then?" Smudge asked.

"He hasn't been keeping me anywhere." She'd snapped out her reply before realising Smudge hadn't meant to imply anything and was just wondering where she was from. "I live in London, but I'm staying with my aunt, Jayne Tilbury, for a while," she explained, guessing some of them might know Jayne.

"Oh!" Phil said as though the answer had solved a problem that had been worrying him.

"Couldn't anything persuade you to stick around?" Jake asked.

"Maybe, I..." If it was what his gorgeous team-mate wanted, he could persuade her, but that was hardly the time to say so. She felt herself blush.

Duncan seemed amused by the conversation, but came to her rescue, sort of. "Mud should do it. Leah's good at getting stuck in the stuff."

Fortunately the quiz started at that point. Everyone

was quiet during each round of the quiz. Teams conferred in whispers. Leah was able to impress them with her knowledge of geography, PG Wodehouse novels and ability to solve anagrams. Duncan answered as many questions as she could and the others all had something useful to contribute. Their final score was just two points short of a full house and one point behind the teams tied on first place.

The draw bizarrely, seemed to make everyone extremely happy.

"It's another rollover," Duncan explained. "That's the ninth in a row and means the prize fund is now impressively high and the team who eventually win will be almost legendary."

"Why don't you just have a tie-breaker?" Leah asked as they walked out to Duncan's car.

"It's a local tradition, going back to when licensing laws first came in apparently. The story goes that the local police officer was in a team who tied and then got the correct answer in the tie-breaker, but not till after time had been called. The opposing team said as the pub was officially closed, he couldn't claim his prize. Another version says he gave the wrong answer, again just after time. Either way, there was some heated discussion about whether the prize should be awarded and the landlord declared the contest invalid and banned tie-break questions. So now we never have them."

Leah smiled as she remembered a phrase she'd used with Jayne on several occasions.

"What's that expression for?" Duncan asked.

"I was just thinking that you country people are weird," she admitted.

"Unlike townies who drive themselves to the gym for exercise, buy coats and shoes that can't be worn in the rain and get raised blood pressure if the internet runs slowly for ten minutes?"

"Have you been practising that retort?"

"Yes. I guess it needs more practice with special attention to spontaneity?"

"No. It works just fine as it is."

He hugged her and bent his head for a kiss but drew back when the rest of their team, who'd followed them out of the pub, cheered and clapped.

"Let's go," Duncan said and opened the car door for her.

Leah had enjoyed herself so much, she'd forgotten about Jayne's medical worries and scheduled hospital visit. On the drive home, she felt guilty about that and lapsed into silence. That didn't help as she remembered how everyone who'd spoken to Duncan had used his name without a trace of hesitation and proved how wrong she'd been to suspect him of using it to hide his real identity. Even someone like Gilmore-Bunce wasn't likely to have the power to make an entire pub full of people pretend he was really a charming farm worker.

There were more lights on at Primrose Cottage when they got back than when they'd left, but no sign of Jim's car. A pity because that meant Jayne was home but hadn't invited him in for coffee. Duncan walked Leah to the door before kissing her cheek.

She reached for his hand. "Duncan?"

He turned back.

"Sorry if I've been quiet. Got a lot on my mind."

He gave her a hug. "I know, but Jayne will be fine, you'll cope brilliantly and I'm here if you need me." He kissed her again, not passionately, but it was a proper kiss. "If you need anything while Jayne's in hospital, don't hesitate to call."

"Thanks, I'll hold you to that."

Tarragon got slowly to his feet when Leah came in, as though pointing out he'd have been fast asleep if it hadn't been his duty to get up and greet those people who insisted on staying out late. His mistress had sensibly gone to bed already. Leah hoped she was sleeping soundly, not lying awake worrying about her medical tests scheduled for the following day. Outside Jayne's bedroom door, Leah whispered 'goodnight' but got no reply.

The following morning Jayne was in a much more optimistic mood than she had been for days. Leah felt better too. She was reasonably confident she could cope with looking after the smallholding for the day and things were going well between her and Duncan.

Leah had expected to be calming Jayne's nerves. Instead she was listening to her sing very badly as she fried eggs and bacon.

"Good night was it?" Leah asked, teasingly.

"Yes, actually. Jim was good fun and the food was very nice."

"Good. And?"

"And I'm going into hospital today. It's too late to back out, isn't it?"

Leah nodded. "Absolutely."

"In a few hours, they'll have done the tests and I'll know the worst. How stupid will I feel if I get myself hysterical and it turns out I've just got a boil on my bum?"

"Pretty silly, although I think your own doctor would have diagnosed a boil."

"True, that's just the example Jim gave me. He searched the internet for pains in the bum."

"I bet he got thousands of very odd results!"

Jayne grinned. "Yes, apparently he did. But even when he looked at proper medical conditions he found dozens of different things. He admitted none of them actually seemed fun, but he also said he didn't find any there weren't any possible treatment options for."

Leah nodded in agreement. She was a little hurt

that Jayne hadn't seemed so convinced when she'd said much the same thing, but didn't show it. "I'm sure he's right."

"He said to assure you that you can phone him anytime if you have a problem or want advice or anything. He'll have his phone with him even when he's at work. Said he'd much rather chat to you than do his job, so not to worry about bothering him."

"That's nice of him."

"Anyone else I've listed will be the same, they know you're not used to all this and won't mind if you call anytime about anything."

"Good, but hopefully I won't need to."

Jayne placed a huge cooked breakfast in front of Leah.

"Are you expecting me to eat all of this?"

"Yes. I put enough bacon in for both of us without thinking. Still as you'll be working for both of us, you'll need plenty of energy."

A huge bouquet arrived just a few minutes before they'd planned to leave for the hospital. The flowers were for Jayne.

"Gosh, what did happen last night?" Leah asked.

"I don't think these are from Jim." Jayne opened the card.

"Well?"

"G-B."

"Why's he sent flowers?" She couldn't help the suspicious tone in her voice.

"To be nice? He says he hopes everything goes well for me and that if there's anything he can do to help, I'm to let him know."

"Oh and he'll rush over and feed the chickens will he?"

"No. I expect he'd send Duncan. Do you disapprove of that?"

She didn't, of course. She really had to get out of her stupid habit of thinking the worst of the man for no good reason.

"He's just being nice, Leah." Jayne spoke as though trying to reason with a three-year old.

"I suppose, but it's good business sense too. If the smallholding goes bust, he'll lose out too."

Jayne laughed. "I'll just stick these in the sink with some water. Can you sort them out properly once you've dropped me off?"

"Sure."

Jayne didn't allow Leah to come into the hospital. "Just drop me off here. I've got plenty of time to find the right place and I promise not to back out now."

"It doesn't seem right just to leave you."

"Go! I'll give you a call when I'm ready to be picked up. If you don't go soon, you'll still be on the way back when I ring."

"All right. I can tell when I'm not wanted."

During the drive back, her phone beeped to tell her she had a text. She waited until she'd parked outside Primrose Cottage before reading it. The message was from Duncan.

'Betcha nothing has gone wrong yet x'.

Like a schoolgirl with a crush, she stroked the x on the screen, then touched her finger to her lips.

Leah typed a message. 'Course not. proper farmer me x x x'. She deleted the final two x's before she sent it.

Arranging Jayne's flowers was Leah's most difficult task for the rest of the day. She fed the pigs and sheep, collected the eggs, checked on Rosepetal and milked Rosemary, but although some of the tasks were hard work, they were all things she'd practised several times and could now do confidently. She'd arranged flowers before, but never such a huge amount. Leah did the best she could to make the flowers look as attractive as possible for Jayne's return.

Throughout the day, Leah checked her phone and looked at Rosepetal. There was no news from Jayne, Duncan hadn't called and she couldn't think of an excuse to ring him. The heifer seemed to be getting a bit fidgety. That was probably due to repeated visits from Leah, who kept feeling her udder. She couldn't really tell if there was any change. She knew the more often she tried the less likely she was to notice a difference, but still couldn't help herself.

Leah typed out another text to Duncan saying everything was OK, but didn't send it. He'd said to call if she wanted him. She did, but not for anything connected to the farm.

At six, Leah's phone rang. It was Jim calling to see if there was any news.

"No, sorry. Perhaps I should call her?"

"Don't worry, you'd have heard if there was a problem. Everything OK there?"

"Yes fine. Don't you worry either. You'll hear from me if there's a problem here!"

Leah checked Rosepetal again before making her supper. The heifer seemed no different. Jayne called as Leah filled a pan with water.

"I'm fine. Sorry I couldn't call before."

"No problem. I'll come and get you now."

"No, they're keeping me in tonight."

"Why? What? ..."

"It's good news, Leah. They found the cause of the problem. Just a cyst."

"And they can remove it?"

"They already have, that's why I'm still here. The anaesthetic didn't agree with me. That's it, Leah, all done!"

"That's fantastic news!"

"Yes, I can't quite believe it. Is everything OK there? Rosepetal?"

"Everything's fine. I'll go and check her again after I've eaten, but I don't think she'll calve before you're back."

"Good. Could you let Jim know? I just want to sleep now."

"Yes, of course."

Leah rang Jim to let him know his boil on the bum theory had been almost correct, then made herself a quick meal of spaghetti with cheese sauce. Once she'd eaten, she went back to check Rosepetal again. There was no signs of her going into labour then, nor at seven-thirty, or eight or eight-thirty. At nine, Leah was convinced that something was happening and stopped to watch. By ten she was cold and it looked like Rosepetal was asleep, so she gave up and went to bed.

She woke in the night convinced something was wrong.

Tarragon was asleep in his bed and didn't stir as she went by. Leah pulled a coat over her pyjamas and put bare feet into her wellies. As she stepped out the front door, Tarragon darted through. She smiled. It didn't seem quite so bad to be up in the middle of the night if she wasn't the only one.

Rosepetal lay on the straw, breathing hard. As

Leah watched, she gave what was definitely a push.

"Sit boy." Leah told the dog. She let herself in with Rosepetal, leaving the dog outside.

The heifer seemed calm and there were no signs she'd been thrashing around in the straw. Leah took a look behind to see if there was any sign of a calf emerging. There wasn't anything, but Rosepetal gave another push. She was definitely in the process of giving birth, but probably only just started. From what Duncan told her, the calf might not arrive for hours.

Leah was very cold. She couldn't stay out all that time in just her pjs, thin coat and wellies. A glance at her watch showed it was only three-thirty; far too early to call Duncan unless it had been a real emergency. She went in to put on more suitable clothing and warm up. She'd intended to just rest on the bed for half an hour but went back to sleep. When she woke again it was after five.

The head of the calf was already out. She could see both front feet too. Rosepetal gave a great heave and more of the slimy calf slithered out. She could see all of its rib cage. Rosemary got to her feet, leaving the calf wriggling on the ground. Immediately she turned to lick it. Leah just watched, feeling ridiculously proud. She'd done nothing to help, but maybe leaving the cow to get on with things and getting some sleep was the best thing she could have done.

Her impulse was to send Duncan a text, but really

it should be Jayne who knew first. Seeing the healthy calf was a huge relief and Leah felt full of energy. Despite several visits to watch the new calf, she had everything done in time to eat breakfast and shower before Jayne rang to say she was ready to leave hospital.

Jayne didn't want to talk about her procedure. "It's over, I just want to forget it. I'm fine, I promise. I'll need to take it easy for a while and I've got a sheet of instructions and half a chemist's shop, but it's all over." She began to cry.

Leah hugged her. "What is it?"

"I'm going to be OK. I'm actually going to be OK."

"Normally I'm not one to gloat, but told you so."

"You did, now get me out of here."

"How's everything going with you?" Jayne asked as they left the hospital grounds.

"Oh fine. Rosemary gave two and a quarter gallons of milk, I collected thirty-eight eggs oh and delivered one calf. Not a bad morning?"

Jayne gasped, but recovered quickly and continued in the same matter of fact tone Leah had used, "Not bad at all. By the look of you everything went OK?"

"Yes. Actually I'm exaggerating to say I delivered him."

"It's a bull?"

"Er, well actually I don't know." It hadn't even occurred to her to check. "I just thought it looked like one. It's nearly all black. He seems lively. Nowhere near as big as the one I saw at Home Farm though."

"He wouldn't be, because of the breed."

Jayne insisted on taking a look at the new arrival before going into the house. The calf was indeed a bull and Jayne was pleased with him. She was pleased with everything Leah had done and incredibly proud of her. Leah knew that because Jayne kept saying so.

"I didn't do much really and nothing at all about the calf."

"Did Duncan come and help?"

"No, I didn't need him."

"Shame."

"Yes. Er, I mean no. It's good Rospetal didn't have too much trouble and I didn't have to disturb him."

"Hmm. I think I'd better pick some herbs."

"Are you going to make yourself a herbal remedy?"

"Something like that."

Leah persuaded Jayne to go inside. Tarragon almost turned cartwheels in his excitement at having his mistress home. Jayne winced slightly as she bent to make a fuss of him.

"Are you OK?" Leah asked.

"Fine, honestly. I think I feel worse from the stiffness of lying about on a bed all day than from the procedure itself. You go and pick my herbs and I'll bake some cakes in case we get visitors."

It sounded as though she were hoping for visitors. Leah selected Duncan's number on her mobile as she walked to the herb garden. She felt guilty before she made the call; it wasn't for Jayne's benefit she wanted him to come. Instead, she tried calling Jim, but found his number engaged. She hoped that meant Jayne was calling him herself.

Her phone rang as she returned with the violet flowers, thyme, sage and rosemary Jayne wanted. It was Duncan.

"How's Jayne?"

"She's fine. I've just brought her back from the hospital, but she wouldn't go in until she'd seen Rosepetal's calf."

"She's had it?"

She'd thought so much about Duncan's advice while the calf was born and been thinking rather a lot about him in general that she'd forgotten he didn't actually know.

"Yes, last night. It really helped me having seen other calves born. Thanks so much for your help."

"You managed all on your own?" He sounded impressed.

"Well, Rosepetal should take some of the credit,"

191

she laughed.

"I suppose, but still I'm very proud of you. Can I come over and see the calf? I don't want to disturb Jayne though."

"Of course you can come over. Jayne will be very happy to see you." Jayne wasn't the only one.

She went in.

"Hope you're making plenty of cakes, because I think Duncan will be over later."

"Oh good, so will Jim."

They grinned at each other.

"You've done a fabulous job with the flowers, lovey. I don't want to spoil them, but I could really do with some red rose petals. Would you mind if we took one rose out?"

"Of course not, they're your flowers!"

Jim and Duncan arrived at the same time that evening. Jim brought daffodils and chocolates for Jayne.

"Of course, nothing's nearly as sweet or pretty as you," he said as he kissed Jayne. "Except maybe this one here," he amended giving Leah a hug.

Duncan brought freesias 'for the midwife'. His peck on her cheek seemed tame compared with Jim's greeting, but she was ridiculously pleased he'd kissed her in front of witnesses.

Jayne insisted everyone drank a cup of the herbal

tea she'd brewed. Neither man looked particularly keen, but they did as they were told.

"This is a different one, what's in it?" Leah asked after a few sips.

"Lavender, violets, rose petals."

"Is it in honour of the calf?" Jim asked.

"No. Talking of the calf though, Duncan must want to see it. Show him, Leah."

"OK."

"Drink up then."

Leah didn't know if Jayne was keen to get her and Duncan alone, or if she wanted some time alone with Jim, but was happy to go along with her wishes either way. She and Duncan gulped down their tea and went out.

Duncan took her hand as they walked across the yard and asked her to tell him all about the birth. He seemed impressed with the calm way she'd coped and Leah couldn't help grinning at his praise. She'd wanted to prove to him she was capable around animals and she'd achieved that by falling asleep during a calving.

"Looks like they're both doing great," Duncan said.

"He's so cute, isn't he?"

"Um hmm."

"It's OK, I know his eventual fate will be the same as the orphan lambs. I'm just in denial about it for now and at least I know he'll have a good life up until then."

"We'll make a farmer out of you yet." He put his arm around her.

"Maybe. I'm enjoying the work far more than I ever thought I would."

Was there a reason he seemed to be wondering if life on a farm would suit her?

"And I love all the animals too. I'm not even scared of big cows now, although I must admit I prefer the smaller ones."

"Smaller breeds, or calves?"

"Calves, really I suppose I meant. All baby animals are cute though, aren't they? Lambs, piglets, chicks."

"What about humans?"

Was he just making conversation, or wondering about her future? Adam had never asked how she felt about a family. Duncan was nothing like Adam.

"I like them too. Toddlers are cute, babies not so much, but I expect I'll feel differently about my own."

"I expect so. I imagine you'd make a great mum."

Leah wondered what were the chances of him finding out.

After that Duncan spent most of the half hour they were outside, cuddling Leah as they watched the cow and her calf, neither of whom did anything much. To her, that seemed a very good use of everyone's time. Eventually and reluctantly, she said that maybe they should go back in.

"All right, but come out with me tomorrow night?"

"I'd love to, but I'm not sure about leaving Jayne. Can I call and let you know?"

He nodded his agreement before giving her the gentlest of kisses.

Chapter 11

"What time is it?" a bleary eyed Jayne asked as she wandered into the kitchen.

"Just after ten." Leah slid bacon into the frying pan.

"Why on earth didn't you wake me?"

"Because you're supposed to be resting. Don't worry, the animals are all fed and I've milked Rosemary."

"Thank you, but..."

"I'll just do the eggs. Pour the tea will you?"

Jayne did as she was asked. "I love you, did I tell you that?" she said when Leah placed a plate of food in front of her.

"Hospital food not up to much?"

"No, but I'm not just grateful for the breakfast."

"I know. How are you feeling today? Up to walking round and telling me what needs doing and how to do it?"

"Absolutely."

After a few hours, Jayne said she was so exhausted from witnessing Leah's energy that she was almost ready to go back to bed.

"Go and have a nap if you like."

"No, I won't sleep tonight if I do. I'll just have a really early night."

"In that case, I might go out, if you don't mind being left on your own?"

"Not if it's Duncan taking you out, I don't."

Leah confessed to feeling a bit tired herself when she rang Duncan.

"How about a quiet drink then? Or I could come round and see you, just chat."

"That sounds nice."

When Jayne heard of that plan, she made up another pot of her herb tea before she went to bed. "Just pour on the hot water, lovey."

Leah and Duncan cuddled on the sofa in front of the fire with Tarragon sprawled over their feet. It felt so good to just relax against him and talk about nothing in particular. She was happy just to be with him and didn't feel the need to listen to music or try to impress him or be entertained. Any doubts that he might be bored soon vanished.

He whispered, "This is nice, just being with you."

She kissed his cheek. "Yes, cosy." She sighed contentedly, imagining what it would feel like to snuggle up in bed with Duncan after a hard day farming.

"Would you like some more of Jayne's herb tea, or a coffee or something?"

"Will it take long to make the tea?"

"As long as it takes the kettle to boil."

"I'll have that then, but don't put too much water in. I don't want you away from my side for too long."

Leah didn't want to be away from him for long either. Her left side felt cold when she moved away from Duncan. She didn't even want to think about him going home at the end of the evening.

She refilled the pot and carried it back in.

Leah allowed her fingers to brush against his as she handed him his drink, then she put hers on the table and wriggled as close to him as she could without actually sitting in his lap.

"What is this stuff for, do you know?" he asked.

"For?"

"Yes. Didn't you say she usually make teas for a particular purpose? Curing colds, or to help you sleep or whatever."

"That's true. I don't know about this one. Maybe it's a relaxing one? I do feel very relaxed." To prove her point, she put her arms round him and rested her head against his chest. She could hear his heart thudding in his chest.

He gave her a squeeze. "That's good." He stroked her hair.

"What about you? Are you relaxed?"

"I wouldn't say that exactly, but I'm happy to be here with you."

Either the tea, hard work, the warm fire, or her contentment meant Leah fell asleep. She woke with a start.

"Sorry, " Duncan whispered. "I didn't mean to wake you, but my arm was going numb."

After a second she realised where she was. "What time is it?"

"Late. I think I should go."

"Oh." Even to her that sounded as pitiful as a child who'd just had his favourite teddy taken away.

Duncan gave a low chuckle. "Going to be able to get up those stairs on your own, or shall I carry you?"

She was tempted to say she needed help, but just managed to stop herself in time.

His kiss goodnight made her wish she hadn't shown such self restraint.

"Leah, I've got to go away for a couple of days. I'm not sure exactly how long for. Can I ring and let you know and take you to dinner as soon as I'm back."

"OK. Don't be gone too long. I don't want to be away from your side..." She was too sleepy to continue, but he hugged her as though he understood and promised to be back soon.

The following morning as she cooked breakfast,

Leah asked about the tea.

"I told you, lavender and violets and..."

"Yes, but what is it for?"

"Er, to drink?"

"Jayne, tell me!"

Jayne fetched a notebook, leafed through it and handed it to Leah.

She scanned down the page, noting the ingredients were just as Jayne had said. Then she saw the name of the recipe. 'Herb tea - Love Potion'.

"Jayne!"

"Careful lovey, you don't want to burn the eggs."

Leah rescued the breakfast and served it. "It can't work, can it? A love potion?"

Jayne shrugged. "Possibly not, but it can't do any harm."

"No? You and Jim both drank a couple of cups the other day."

"Well there you go then."

Leah wasn't sure if she was being reassured the herbal brew had no effect, or that Jayne was suggesting it worked.

"Talking of Jim, I've invited him to lunch on Sunday."

"OK, I'll make myself scarce."

"No, don't do that!"

"I don't mind, honestly."

"I do. I like Jim, but I'm not sure if I want to be more than friends."

"OK, I understand." That sounded just the way Leah had kidded herself she felt about Duncan. She now knew she wanted a lot more than friendship from him and decided it was time to prove to herself that she could adapt to life away from London.

Leah threw herself into farm work more enthusiastically than ever. It was she, directed by Jayne, who collected the orphan lambs from Home Farm. It was a little disappointing not to see Duncan, but as she enjoyed demonstrating her competence to him, it was probably just as well he didn't see her become a gooey mess at the sight of the cute little creatures. She soon had them settled into their new accommodation and it seemed they grew bigger by the hour.

The other tasks seemed much easier than when she'd first started, because Leah was now so much stronger and fitter than she'd been in London. She felt emotionally stronger and more confident too, no longer needing the approval of Adam or anyone else before she made a decision. Perhaps if she'd felt that way at the start of her relationship with him, things would have been much better between them. Often Adam had little choice but to do as he wanted, because Leah hadn't been assertive enough to make her own wishes known. She wouldn't make that mistake with Duncan.

A lorry pulled into the yard and Leah went to see what the driver wanted.

"I'm Dave, I've come for the pigs, love," he explained.

"Oh, yes of course. I'll get Jayne."

Leah had known the oldest pen of pigs were due to go to slaughter that day, but had deliberately put the thought from her mind. She had a feeling she wouldn't be wanting bacon for breakfast in the morning.

The pigs walked up into the lorry with no trouble, which just made Leah feel worse.

"Doesn't it make you sad?" she asked once the lorry had driven away. "When your animals go off to be turned into meat?"

"A bit, yes but I can't keep them all."

"No, of course not."

Jayne had a call that afternoon. She reacted as though the news were good, then asked the caller to, "Hold on a second."

"It's Dave, the chap who took the pigs. A mate of his has some little ones to sell and Dave said he'll keep them for me if I'm interested. I was going to wait for a while before getting another batch, but I think we could handle them now, couldn't we?"

As Jayne negotiated arrangements for getting the piglets, Leah reflected on the 'we'. Obviously Jayne now thought of them as a team. Leah would like to make that a reality.

She was pleased with how well she coped with life and work on the farm. The lifestyle appealed to her and not just because it meant she was near Duncan. Eventually Leah would have the money from her share of the flat she'd bought with Adam. She could go into partnership with Jayne. Maybe between them they'd have enough to buy Primrose Cottage and the small farm. That should save loads on rent and would mean Jayne no longer had to rely on Oliver Gilmore-Bunce. Leah made the suggestion to Jayne.

"I'd love to have you here permanently, lovey, but you need to think a bit more before deciding on a partnership. Even if we did really well we wouldn't make a lot of money and the work never stops. I know you're hard working and reliable, but at the moment it's all still a novelty for you. We'd need to look carefully at the finances too. Best not to rush into anything."

"You're right, of course, I haven't properly thought it out. I will do, but you like the idea in theory?"

"I like the idea of you moving away from London and setting up home down here very much."

"That's what I want. I've been wondering what to do about work. I don't want to stay even if the company wants me back, which I'm not sure it does. It seems pretty clear I'm not fully trusted and that someone doesn't want me there. If I just hand in my

203

notice before my name is cleared it might look as though I'm admitting guilt. If they don't hurry up and sort things out, I could claim compensation for constructive dismissal, according to my legal advisor. Oh, it's all such a mess, I just want out of it."

"They're still paying you, aren't they?"

"Yes."

"Then do nothing for now. They owe you that for not trusting you and any money you save now will come in handy later."

Leah nodded. "Wouldn't it be great if we could buy this place?"

"We can't, lovey. G-B can't sell. A legal thing was set up by his great grandfather which says Primrose Cottage and the surrounding land can't be sold out of the Gilmore-Bunce family."

"Oh, that's a shame."

"Not really. Ownership wouldn't be so great. The rent doesn't cover the repairs. Because it's a listed building it's very expensive and takes ages, that's why things can't always be fixed straight away."

That sounded like a con to Leah.

"Are you sure? You're paying more a month than a year's mortgage on my flat in London. I know this is bigger, but prices are cheaper here."

"I'd forgotten how good you are with the financial and computer stuff. You must have seen the figures when you were helping me and remembered."

"Yes. Sorry, I didn't mean to pry."

"You weren't, silly. If there was anything I didn't want you seeing, I'd have said, but I don't have any secrets from you. There's one little detail I think you missed though."

"What's that?" It couldn't have been a decimal point in the wrong place, Leah didn't make mistakes like that.

"My rent is annual."

"Oh!"

That changed things. How had she made such a mistake? For a moment, she worried the problem with Gilmore-Bunce's accounts could really have been her fault. That wasn't possible though. Even if she had made such a mistake, the money wouldn't have gone missing and the error would soon have been noticed.

Leah sighed. Her stupid hatred of Oliver Gilmore-Bunce had become such a habit she'd simply expected to see he was overcharging Jayne and so had misinterpreted the figures to back up her prejudice. He simply wasn't such a bad landlord as she'd originally thought. Maybe she was going soft now she'd escaped from The City, but she was having a tough time remembering how much she'd hated him. Her past life just didn't seem important anymore.

"So, did you miss me?" Duncan asked once they'd ordered their food.

"Why, have you been away?" She knew she was wasting her time trying to play it cool, because the way she'd thrown herself into his arms when he'd arrived at Primrose Cottage had given her away completely.

His gentle laugh confirmed that. He was even better looking when he laughed. The few laughter lines around his eyes showed he laughed a lot and also hinted he'd still be a handsome man in the years to come.

It had been a shock to see Duncan all dressed up in a suit, but he'd explained he had to pass by on his way home and couldn't wait to see her. For a second, seeing his formal clothing, Leah was reminded of Adam. He'd always looked good in a suit. Duncan did too, but then he'd probably look good in anything. Adam always looked half naked and uncomfortable without a tie and jacket. Half naked would probably be another good look for Duncan.

Leah gave herself a mental shake and remembered she had other things to think about, such as how to drop casually into the conversation that she was considering making her move from London permanent. As Jayne had suggested she should, Leah thought hard about her future and what she wanted to do. She realised a lot depended on how her relationship with Duncan developed. The future she dreamed of included having him by her side. He seemed keen now, but she'd told him her visit to Winkleigh Marsh was only temporary. Would he lose interest if she became a permanent fixture?

"Penny for them?" Duncan said.

"Oh, I was just thinking..." she blushed. It wouldn't exactly be casual to say she was wondering what he'd wear to their wedding. Even less subtle to mention she'd been daydreaming about feeding orphan lambs with children who looked just like him and called her Mummy. "Um, about families."

"You planning to introduce me to your parents?"

She grinned. Perhaps his thoughts weren't so different from hers.

"They're living in New Zealand at the moment. Dad's a diplomat so he's away more than he's in England. They're hoping to come and stay with Jayne for a few weeks in the summer. I'll be happy to introduce you then." That was easy, she'd effortlessly showed she intended to still be there in the summer and still be seeing him.

"I look forward to it."

"What about yours? Are you going to introduce me to them?" Maybe that wasn't casual enough, there was a worried look on his face.

"I don't know. Dad's not at all well and Mum... We'll see shall we?"

She reached over and squeezed his hand. "I'm so

sorry. Is that where you've been, visiting them?"

He nodded, the worried look deepened. Leah couldn't think how to comfort him, but after a moment he gave an answering squeeze and a small smile.

"I did mention you actually. Dad asked if you were as pretty as May. She'd have been your gran wouldn't she?"

"That's right."

Their food arrived at that moment, meaning Leah couldn't find out how he'd answered his dad's question without it seeming she was fishing for compliments. Appropriately enough, the meal was beautiful. Even in London she'd not seen food better presented. Her warm camembert tart on its bed of salad would have been attractive even without the redcurrant sauce drizzled into heart shapes around the edge of the plate. It was almost too pretty to eat. Almost.

She looked up to see Duncan too was enjoying his food. Leah was glad he had an appetite at least as healthy as her own. She always felt so greedy around people who just picked at their food.

"Talking of family, how's Jayne doing? By the look of her this afternoon she's recovering well."

"Yes, she's absolutely fine. She dosed herself up with some of her herbal remedies, but she's followed all the medical advice too. She goes to bed a bit earlier than she used to, but I think she only stayed up late before because she was worried. She's almost completely back to normal now."

"Really?" He gave a mock shocked look.

"Normal for Jayne, I meant."

"That's OK then." He grinned.

When they'd finished their food he said, "Did you find out what that herbal tea she made us drink was for?"

"Er, yes."

"What?"

"It was a love potion, apparently."

"Ah."

Leah concentrated on pouring wine in order to avoid meeting his gaze.

"And she goes to bed early, you say?"

"Yes, if you come in for coffee we'll just have Tarragon for a chaperone." She could feel herself blush so it probably didn't matter much that she was finding it hard to sound casual.

The second course arrived right on cue. It was just as artistically presented and just as delicious as the starter. They didn't talk much, but his expression whenever she glanced at him told her all she needed to know.

"Would you care to see the dessert menu?" the waiter asked.

For the first time in her life, Leah wanted to say 'no'. The food was wonderful, but no competition for what she hoped would happen after Duncan drove her home.

"Please," Duncan said. He gave her a teasing smile. "You weren't in a hurry to get away, were you, Leah?"

"Well, I..."

"If I take you back too soon Jayne might be worried you haven't eaten enough and get up to make you a snack."

"In that case, I'm not in a hurry, no."

The crème brûlée was worth savouring, so the delay wasn't too agonising.

Duncan declined the waiter's offer of coffee. "I think we'd rather have violet tea."

"I'm sorry, sir I don't think we serve that."

"Not to worry, I know a place that does."

The waiter smiled to show he knew a joke had been made even if he had no idea what had made Leah blush and dissolve into giggles.

Duncan opened the car door for her, but he pulled her close before she could get in. "What am I going to do with you, Leah?"

She was sure it was a rhetorical question, but kissed him anyway as a clue to the answer. He held her tight as he kissed her back. Leah moaned and felt herself go limp in his arms.

"Get in the car, woman," he muttered huskily as he released her.

He drove carefully, but gave the impression of being frustrated with the slow speed made necessary by the narrow lanes and tight corners. Duncan braked sharply outside Primrose Cottage to avoid the car parked right by the turning into the yard.

Leah guessed he said something uncomplimentary about the lack of consideration shown by the driver, but she wasn't really listening. She was concentrating on the car, willing it not to be one she recognised.

By the time Duncan had parked, the driver of the other vehicle had followed them, on foot, into the yard. Before Duncan had switched off the engine, Leah wrenched open the door and jumped out. Her legs felt weak and her high heeled sandals were hardly appropriate for the farmyard, but she forced herself to stride with apparent confidence towards the visitor.

"What are you doing here?" she hissed. How many times had she asked him to bring her to visit Jayne and been fobbed off with feeble excuses? Then, after she'd fled to the comfort of Primrose Cottage after her troubles at work she'd practically begged him to come and he'd cut her off with a reminder they were finished. Now, just when she least wanted to see him, he turned up.

211

"Leah, I need to talk to you," Adam said.

"I don't have anything to say to you." She did, but none of it was polite and it no longer seemed important.

"Leah, what's happening?" Duncan asked.

"Nothing. He's just going."

Both men glared at each other. If either had ever shown any violent tendencies, she'd have been sure they were about to fight. As it was, it still seemed possible they might.

Leah stepped between them and turned to Duncan. "He was the someone in London, but it's all over now."

"No it isn't," Adam insisted. "Leah, I made a terrible mistake. I must talk to you, please let me explain."

"It's too late," Leah said. She didn't know if the tears forming in her eyes were from frustration, anger or regret.

"It doesn't have to be. I love you."

Leah gasped. Never before had he said he loved her without being prompted. Never before had he said it in front of anyone else. Could he really mean it?

"Yeah and proved it by abandoning her when she needed you most?" Duncan asked.

"I don't have to prove myself to you," Adam said.

"No, only to Leah and I think you've already done that." Duncan stepped close. "I don't want to leave you with him, Leah, but I think I'd better let you listen to what he's got to say. You might regret it if you don't and I want you to be completely sure how you feel. Call me later, eh?" He squeezed her tight, kissed her gently on the mouth, then walked away.

Chapter 12

"Well, go on then. Explain," Leah hissed at Adam. She didn't really want to hear his answer any more than she wanted to hear the sounds telling her Duncan was turning his car and driving away from her, but it was clear she was going to have to.

Adam approached as though he wanted to kiss her.

She took a step back. "You made a terrible mistake, you said?"

"Leah, it's so good to see you."

"If you're so pleased to see me now, why didn't you come here with me, or visit when I asked you to? Why didn't you call me or reply to my messages and texts?"

"I should have. I'm sorry. Things have been very difficult for me at work and I've missed you."

He tried again to reach out for her. Again she moved away.

"Things were rather difficult for me at work if you remember, but you weren't there to support me."

"I know, I know. I should have been. I'm so sorry." He stepped closer. When Leah stepped back again he looked surprised. Had she always been so easy for him to talk round, she wondered.

"Could we possibly go inside? I've had a long drive up here and when I got here your aunt didn't seem very pleased to see me."

"Any reason why she should?" It wasn't nice of her, but she was pleased he'd had to wait for nothing and enjoyed seeing him squirm. So often in the past he'd made her feel small in front of his friends or made her afraid to say what she thought for fear of causing an argument. It might do him good to know how it felt to be nervous about what you said and unsure of how the other person would react.

"No, no of course not but well, I need the toilet."

"And Jayne wouldn't let you in?" Leah was suspicious. It didn't seem likely that Jayne would be so inhospitable. Maybe Adam was trying to make it seem someone other than he was in the wrong. He was good at that.

"When she explained you were out, I said I'd wait in the car. The lights went off soon after, so I didn't like to disturb her."

Adam uncomfortable and at a disadvantage was such a novelty for Leah she almost felt sorry for him.

"You can use the toilet, but then you've got a long drive back. I've got nothing to say to you."

When Adam emerged from the bathroom he said he had something for her in the car. "If I fetch it, will you let me back in?"

"All right."

She didn't want the flowers or whatever he had bought, but she was curious to see what he thought might win her round.

He returned with a gorgeous bouquet of flowers. Leah didn't accept them from him but she allowed him to follow her into the living room.

"Does that dog bite?" he asked when he spotted Tarragon sprawled in front of the dying fire.

"No, of course not."

Tarragon greeted Leah in rather a half-hearted way. She wasn't surprised, he wasn't used to being awake at this time of night. She was surprised though when the dog completely ignored Adam.

Adam tried again to present the flowers. When she still didn't take them he put them on the coffee table and launched into a long, complicated apology for his terrible behaviour. Watching him squirm lost its novelty value and Leah felt genuinely sorry for him. She didn't want to be on bad terms with anyone and as they still had to sort out about the flat she'd have to speak to him again. It would be so much better if they could be friendly.

"Thank you for the flowers, they're lovely."

"You're welcome. I should have bought you flowers more often in the past. I rather took you for granted, didn't I?"

"Yes." Friendly was one thing, she wasn't prepared

to lie to save his feelings.

"Things will be different now, I promise."

"Adam, I..." She trailed off as he dropped to one knee.

"Leah, will you marry me?"

He pulled a tiny box from his jacket pocket and offered it to her. She was so shocked she took it without a word and opened it. Inside was a diamond ring.

Adam took it from her and placed it on her finger. She watched as though it were someone else's hand.

"No pre-nup, Leah. We'll do things just the way you want them. I've missed you so much. I didn't realise how much you meant to me until you'd gone. I thought at first you'd come back, but when you didn't I thought perhaps you'd misinterpreted what I said on the phone and thought I didn't want you back, so I thought I'd come and show you how much I do."

She could have misinterpreted his words, although she didn't think she had. She certainly hadn't misinterpreted his lack of compassion when she'd first been suspended from work nor the nearly two months of silence from him since.

"You don't seem very excited," Adam complained.

So, after saying what he wanted and what he thought, he got around to thinking about her feelings?

He rose to his feet and peered at her face as though

checking for signs of illness.

"It's late and I'm tired and this is all a bit of a shock," she mumbled, moving away from him yet again.

"Yes, of course. I'm sorry. I've done this all the wrong way round, haven't I? I want you to come back to London with me. I'm working hard to clear your name but it would be easier if you were there to answer questions and, of course, I'd be happier if you were back home."

"You've told Prophet Margin about us living together?"

"No, I wouldn't do that without checking with you first. I'll tell them if you want me to."

She shrugged. It no longer mattered. "And you'll meet my family and I'll meet yours?"

"Of course, of course."

She couldn't think straight. Adam was offering everything she'd once thought she wanted. There had been times when she'd cried herself to sleep because he didn't love her enough to want to marry her.

"Come back to London with me tomorrow, Leah. We'll go to the theatre and have dinner at that Italian place you like."

She was tempted. There were things about London she missed and she'd like to collect more clothes from the flat. Perhaps she should give her old life another chance before deciding to make her escape to the country permanent.

"Jim's coming to lunch tomorrow, I said I'd be here."

"Jim? He's not the man you were with tonight."

"No, a friend of Jayne's."

"If it's important to you then we'll stay until after lunch."

"I need to sleep. We get up early here and I'm really tired. I can't think now."

"Of course. Where's the nearest hotel?"

"I've no idea. You'd better stay here tonight."

"But your aunt..."

"It'll be OK." She pointed him in the direction of a bedroom, thankful for Jayne's policy of always keeping a bed made up 'just in case' and left him to it.

He asked if her aunt was old fashioned, but she ignored him. She wasn't ready to let him back into her bed and doubted if she ever would be. She took the ring off before going to bed and replaced it in its box. An engagement ring was another thing she wasn't ready for. She wanted one, but not that one. Not now.

Jayne and Leah put fresh straw in the pigsties ready for the new arrivals on Monday.

Leah said, "I want you to measure them for me, so I know what size they were when they arrived."

219

"Stay here and you'll see for yourself," Jayne said, kicking at the straw to spread it.

"I can't, Jayne. You know I can't. I have to go back to London and make sure that whatever decision I reach is the right one. I've been with Adam over two years. I can't just throw all that away after less than two months down here, not without seeing if it could work. And if it doesn't, then I can finalise everything up there, sort out the sale of the flat or get Adam to buy me out and pack up all my stuff."

"I suppose. I just don't trust him."

"Be fair, you haven't spoken to him except to shut the door in his face last night."

Jayne laughed. "True and I did enjoy that! Pompous creature stood there with a bunch of flowers expecting to be welcomed with open arms."

"Jayne, you're cruel."

"Never denied it. Look out, here he comes."

Adam picked his way across the yard as though getting a speck of mud on his immaculate trousers would give him the plague.

"Good morning, ladies. Lovely day."

"Beautiful," Jayne agreed. "Hello, Adam. I'm sorry we didn't get off to a very good start yesterday. I've not been well lately and that makes me tired and when I'm tired I'm grumpy." She set off towards the chicken run.

Adam followed. "I quite understand. I'm sorry for

disturbing you so late, but once I came to my senses about Leah, I just had to come and see her straight away."

Jayne waved her hand as though to say that didn't matter. "How was the bed? I hope you slept all right?" She held the chicken run door open for Adam to follow her.

"I did, thank you and thank you for putting me up."

Leah stayed outside with Tarragon. She guessed what was coming next and knew some of the chickens had started to go broody. Leah supposed she should stick up for Adam, but she kept quiet and listened to him trying to charm Jayne. Sure enough, he praised the hens and lovely brown eggs and Jayne invited him to collect some. Adam did a pretty good job of stifling his yelp of pain as the broody hen pecked at the strange man stealing her eggs.

Jayne handed Leah the egg basket. "Adam's helped me collect the eggs, isn't that nice?"

"Lovely," Leah agreed, trying to scowl at Jayne without Adam noticing.

"Would you like to see the sheep?" Jayne asked.

"Er, yes," Adam said.

"Good, you can help me with the hay. Leah, you go and get the breakfast started, I'm sure Adam will be hungry when he comes in."

She didn't want to stop Jayne's fun, but enough was enough. "And muddy. Jayne, he hasn't got any

221

boots."

"Oh, what was I thinking? Adam go in with Leah and she'll sort you out a pair. I always keep spares for visitors. That is, if you really do want to see the sheep and don't mind giving me a hand?"

"No. Yes. I mean, I'd like to." Obediently he followed Leah and tried on Jayne's spare boots. The ones Leah borrowed when she'd got stuck in the mud were too small, so he had to borrow some that were too big. Leah wasn't at all sure he'd keep them on his feet in the sticky mud of the sheep paddock.

"Adam, you don't have to do this."

"It's fine. I think your aunt likes me."

Leah didn't have the heart to tell him that was probably a very bad sign.

Neither did she have the heart, when he returned soaking wet and slightly dazed, to ask what happened with the sheep. She just took Adam up to the bathroom then hunted for some clothes he could change into. The best she could find were her tracksuit bottoms and a pale pink sweater. Both were an incredibly tight fit and left quite a bit of his hairy arms and legs exposed, but were better than his ripped trousers and soaking shirt and jacket. At least, Leah supposed he'd think they were. He was always so particular about his appearance and projecting the right image that she didn't think he'd be particularly grateful. She handed them over without a word and went down to see Jayne.

"What on earth did you do to him?"

"Nothing. Didn't need to. He ran away from the ram, grabbed the electric fence and then dived head first into the water trough."

Leah bit her lip. She would not laugh at Adam's misfortune.

"Nice polite boy. He apologised for being a nuisance when I fished him out. He says he likes the farm so maybe you could spend your honeymoon here?"

"Jayne, I don't think..."

"Don't worry, I wouldn't be here. I could go and spend a couple of weeks with your parents in New Zealand. If you timed it right you could be here for when Rosemary calved. I'm sure Adam would like that."

"Like what?" Adam asked nervously.

"Ah! There you are. All nice and clean and ready for your breakfast."

Adam didn't seem particularly hungry. That may have been because Jayne spent the meal explaining how Leah had acted as midwife to Rosepetal and suggesting Adam might like the same experience. The process was a great deal more slimy and hands on than Leah recalled it being in real life.

Adam must have spent some of the two months she'd been away discovering he enjoyed cooking because he enthusiastically volunteered to help peel potatoes and chop carrots and apples. It was either that, or he didn't want to help with any more farm work.

"Good choice," Jayne approved. "You stay in the warm and dry and tell me all about yourself while Leah feeds the orphan lambs."

He made a brave but unconvincing attempt at a smile.

When Jim arrived, Jayne went out to meet him. She must have briefed him about the unexpected guest because he didn't react at all when introduced to a man wearing a pink sweater, incredibly tight tracksuit trousers and slippers shaped like ducklings which were all several sizes too small. He simply said it was a pleasure to meet Adam and clapped him on the back. Although he needed to take two paces to steady himself, Adam didn't actually fall over.

The briefing was thorough enough that Jim didn't kiss Leah more than once and directed most of his flirting toward Jayne. It apparently hadn't covered Leah's return to London though as Jim offered her a job.

"The chap who does the accounts at the feed mill is retiring soon. If you wanted the job you could start when you like and work with him for a while to get you settled in."

"Leah has a job," Adam said.

"In London though, isn't it?"

Adam agreed it was.

"Well she can't be driving down there everyday, can she?" Jim pointed out.

"Thank you, Jim. It's kind of you to think of me."

"Oooh, I think about you a lot." Jim winked. "Be nice having a pretty thing like you about the place."

"Leah can think about it and let you know, can't she?" Jayne asked.

"Oh yes, of course. No rush."

As soon as they'd eaten, Adam suggested Leah should pack.

"I don't think I need to. I still have plenty of clothes in London and I'll be coming back here soon, so I'll need some here." Whatever she decided about her future, she wasn't going to stay away from Winkleigh Marsh for too long at a time and it was best that Adam knew that.

"Fine. Well, we can get going soon then?"

"Wouldn't you like some nice herbal tea before you rush off?" Jayne suggested.

"No, he wouldn't!" Leah said. She wasn't at all sure what Jayne might brew up. "Why don't you make some of that nice violet stuff for you and Jim?"

Jayne grinned. "If you're going off and leaving me then I just might."

"What are you two talking about?" Jim asked.

They didn't explain.

225

Leah wanted to call Duncan and tell him what was happening. She didn't know what she could say though, so just sent a text saying, 'Sorry for last night. I have things to sort out. Speak soon. x' It wasn't good, but hopefully better than leaving without contacting him at all.

During the drive Leah kept her phone switched off. She couldn't speak to Duncan whilst sitting next to Adam.

Adam told her about the investigations he'd been making into the accusations Mr Gilmore-Bunce made about the handling of his investments. To Leah, it seemed almost as though he were talking about people and problems she knew nothing about. Just a few weeks ago clearing her name and regaining her position of trust at Prophet Margin had been almost all she could think about. Now they didn't seem important at all. She tried to snap out of her lethargy and concentrate on what he was saying.

"Is Rachel still involved in the investigations? I haven't heard from her lately."

"Rachel West?"

"Yes, she called me and said she was investigating with you."

"What did you say to her?"

"Not much."

"Best keep it that way. I don't altogether trust her."

Leah hadn't trusted Rachel in the past, but she'd

changed her mind when Rachel told her about the investigation. Perhaps that was some trick of Rachel's? Leah decided to call her tomorrow and say she was back in London. Rachel's reaction to that news might give a clue as to how trustworthy she really was.

"But none of that really matters," Adam said. "What's important is that I have you back with me."

Leah smiled. She'd been thinking that work was more important to him than she was. It was reassuring to hear that wasn't the case.

"Let's go out tonight, see a show. Something funny?" he suggested.

"Yes, good idea."

The comedian they went to see was quite funny, but all his jokes were at someone else's expense. The meal afterwards was fine, but no better than the restaurants Duncan had taken her to and far less substantial than the meals she'd enjoyed with Jayne. Leah found herself wondering where the out of season courgettes and raspberries had been flown in from. Adam was charming, just as he had been when they'd first dated, but the charm now felt a little superficial.

The waiter asked if they'd like coffee and Adam ordered black decaf.

"And for madam?"

"Do you serve anything with violets in?"

"Violets, madam?"

"Don't worry about it. I'll have coffee with lots of caffeine, plenty of sugar and loads of cream."

"Certainly, madam."

"Leah, what's wrong?"

"Wrong? I've changed how I take my coffee, what's wrong with that?"

"It's not just the coffee."

So he had noticed.

"Everything is different, Adam. I don't feel I fit in here anymore."

"Of course you do. Soon you'll be back at work and everything will be just as it was."

Leah shook her head. It wouldn't, even if she wanted it to be.

"Of course it will." He reached out and took the hand she'd clenched around her coffee cup. "I know these last few weeks have been unsettling, but together we can sort things out. Everything will be fine."

"How can it? I'm not trusted at work. Everyone thinks I'm... well, I don't know what, but they won't trust me. Nobody will."

"I trust you. I can prove it too, I'm working on a new investment, I could put it in your name."

Was everything about money with him?

"I don't want to get involved in any new financial

dealings at the moment, Adam."

"No, no, of course not."

She was beginning to wish she'd not returned to London and there was worse to come. She had to spend the night in a one bedroom flat with Adam. She didn't expect she'd sleep well.

"I'll sleep on the sofa," she said when they returned to the flat.

"Don't be ridiculous! We've shared that bed for two years, one more night won't matter."

She didn't answer.

"I'll take the sofa," he said eventually.

Leah was wrong about sleeping. The emotions she'd experienced over the previous twenty-four hours had drained her and she slept until almost eight.

Adam tapped softly on the bedroom door.

"Come in."

"Fancy a coffee?"

She smiled and nodded.

It was relaxing to lie there, waiting for coffee and knowing she didn't have to get up and milk Rosemary or contend with grumpy hens. She recalled the scabs on the back of Adam's hand where he'd been pecked. He hadn't once complained about that. Leah remembered Jayne's account of how he'd managed to get soaking wct. It had seemed funny, but he must have been scared. He hadn't complained about that either, nor about having to wear her clothes at lunch. He must have hated that. He probably hadn't been that pleased by Leah's refusal to wear the engagement ring or share his bed either.

Perhaps she'd misjudged him. He must really want her back and be feeling bad about his earlier neglect of her to go through all that without whinging and expecting praise. He'd been considerate last night, too. Presumably he'd wanted to talk business and be reassured she was back for good. Instead of insisting on that, he'd taken her out. Adam's usual choice of entertainment was an obscure yet serious play or an opera where everyone died after forty minutes of agony, forgiveness or retribution depending on the plot. He'd chosen something far more likely to appeal to her than to him. If he'd actually changed as much as it seemed he had, then maybe they could be happy together.

Chapter 13

Adam brought in two coffees and sat on the bed to drink his.

"Aren't you going to be late for work?" Leah asked.

"No. I'm taking today off. I thought we could go out, spend some time getting to know each other again."

"Oh. Yes, good idea."

They both finished their coffee quickly and Adam took out the cups, saying he'd leave her to get dressed.

When he was gone, Leah checked her phone. There were two missed messages from Duncan and a text which simply read, 'Hi xxx'. She tried sending him a text to explain her return to London. She gave up when she realised she didn't understand herself quite what was happening. In the end she settled for, 'Still trying to sort things out. Will be in touch soon. x'

Leah and Adam spent the day playing tourists in central London. They went to places she'd long wished to visit, but which they'd never found time for previously.

She'd almost forgotten how convenient the tube was for getting to the National Gallery, Natural History Museum and China Town. There were so many interesting places to see in London and so many historic pubs, modern wine bars and an endless array of places to buy every kind of food she could think of. One minute they were in Harrods, the next in a street market. It seemed she could do anything, go anywhere and still be just a short walk or ride from home.

Adam didn't tut when she preferred the pretty paintings to the important ones or say 'don't encourage them' when she dropped a few coins in the hat of buskers who were playing a cheerful tune. He didn't suck in his breath when she ordered food containing fat or sugar. He constantly asked where she wanted to go, what she wanted to do. More amazing still, he listened to her replies and acted on them.

Had he been so kind and considerate when they first dated? She couldn't remember. She did know he hadn't behaved like that during the last year. If she stayed, would it continue?

Duncan returned her text. 'Call me if you need anything. Hope to see you soon. Love Duncan. x'

Adam looked at her as though expecting to be told who the message was from. She said nothing.

That evening Adam took her for cocktails, then to

the theatre. They got back late and Adam did no more than kiss her cheek before she went, alone, into the bedroom.

He brought her coffee before leaving for work. "Where will you go today? Kew Gardens or one of the parks might be pretty now, with all the spring bulbs out."

"Maybe."

He was right, but those places were no prettier than the drifts of primroses, crocus and violets around Jayne's cottage.

"Or the zoo?"

"Don't worry, Adam. I'm sure I can amuse myself until you get home."

"Of course you can. There's so much to do in London."

Lingering over breakfast had little appeal when whole-grain muesli and skimmed milk was the most exciting thing on offer and there was no one to talk to. They hadn't done much talking the previous day. Not about anything important. Nothing to help solve her problem at Prophet Margin or help her decide what to do with her life. The whole day had been false - she'd come to try to sort things out and Adam had acted as though there was nothing to discuss. If he really thought there was nothing wrong, then the two of them had drifted even further apart than she'd

233

realised.

Leah looked around the shops. There were plenty of goods on offer, but nothing she needed or even wanted. Hundreds of people surrounded her in every direction yet she didn't recognise a single face. Entertainment and education opportunities were plentiful, but there was nothing that seemed like a good use of her time. Nothing that couldn't be left until tomorrow. Life was harder on the farm, but there had been a good reason for everything she'd done there. Animals and people had depended on her. In London no one would even notice if she weren't there.

Determined not to waste her time entirely, Leah rang Rachel. Maybe there was news Adam had been reluctant to pass on for fear of spoiling their lovely day yesterday.

Rachel suggested they meet for a coffee. "I could do with getting out the office for a while anyway."

They arranged to meet at an open-air cafe in the park nearest Prophet Margin's offices.

"It's so frustrating, Leah. I'm sure you're innocent and I'm not the only one, but finding evidence is proving to be much harder than I anticipated. One thing I am sure of is that whatever happened wasn't an accident. Things were set up to make it seem you were guilty."

"Great, so someone's got it in for me? No wonder Mr Gilmore-Bunce is so sure I'm guilty."

"I'm not sure he ever did think that, but he certainly doesn't now. You really impressed him."

"How can I have done? I've never even met him, except one time in the office before this all happened and then we didn't speak."

"Are you sure?"

"Adam pointed him out. He certainly looked like your typical snooty rich country gent."

"Adam Ferrand? I wouldn't trust a word that man said. It's probably him who got you into this mess, but that's not what I meant. Are you sure you've not met the client? He contacted us to offer every assistance in clearing your name, those were his words."

Duncan must have put in a good word for her with his relative. How sweet of him and how modest not to have mentioned it to her. With a touch of guilt she realised she'd not said, or thought, anything in Adam's defence.

"What did you say about Adam? You can't really think it was him who stole the money?"

"He's been moving client's money around for no apparent reason. It does look as though he's trying to clear his tracks from something, although it might not be anything to do with your case. Sorry, I really shouldn't have said anything. I admit I don't like the man and I'm biased, but he's certainly up to something."

Leah didn't think it at all likely Adam would steal money from a client. Neither did she think he'd take her diary from her bag, but if he had looked in it, he'd have seen her computer passwords. No, it wasn't possible; she trusted him. Could she trust Rachel though? She'd not been her friend before, maybe she wasn't now?

"I don't really know what to say."

Rachel shrugged. "No. Like I said, I shouldn't have said anything. I don't know why I did really, I don't agree with people being accused with no proof and I don't have any evidence against him."

"We'll forget about it, then?" Leah suggested, although she knew for her it wouldn't be possible.

"OK. Tell me, what's been happening with you? Did you really go off to some horrible old farm?"

"Yes, well I don't think it's horrible, but I have been staying with my aunt on her farm. I enjoy working with the animals."

Rachel grinned. "Prophet Margin's clients are good training for that. Right pigs and cows some of them."

"Real pigs and cows aren't so much trouble," Leah assured her.

"What's the social life like? All Morris Dancing and sacrificing virgins?"

"Only at the weekends. Actually it's pretty good. They do have pubs and restaurants outside of London and people are very friendly. We visit the neighbours and things like that."

"Sounds amazing." Rachel didn't try to hide her sarcasm.

"One of my aunt's neighbours is Chantelle Miller. She threw this fantastic party."

"Chantelle Miller the designer? You're kidding me."

Leah tried to mention some of the famous guests, but Rachel interrupted. "I know, I saw a write up in the paper."

It was Leah's turn to interrupt and she spoke over Rachel. "You can't have done. There weren't any paparazzi, it wasn't the kind of party."

"It wasn't a gossip piece, just a mention in the fashion section along with pictures of your friend's latest designs. You didn't get a mention, but some of the other guests did. By the sound of it, there were some gorgeous men there, did you..."

Leah just grinned, hoping to let Rachel decide for herself what that meant.

"Who? Come on, spill."

"Well, actually it isn't anyone famous, but he is gorgeous."

"So will you be moving to the country to raise chickens and babies?"

"I don't know, Rachel."

"You mean you're actually considering it?"

"Yes, I suppose I am."

After Rachel went back to work, Leah thought about the conversation. She didn't know who to believe. Rachel had seemed to be genuine, but if she was, why was the investigation taking so long and why was Rachel trying to cast blame onto Adam? One thing she did know was that she was seriously considering spending the rest of her life with Duncan. She hadn't known him long, but she was sure they could be happy together and almost sure he felt the same way about her. First though, to be fair to everyone, she had to be sure her relationship with Adam had no future. He'd said he wanted to explain, for them to talk and to sort things out, but that hadn't happened.

She called him at work and said she'd cook dinner that evening.

"What do you fancy? I'll pick up what we need."

"I thought you'd like to go out. There's a great Vietnamese place I've heard about. It's very authentic and everything's ethically sourced."

"I'd rather stay in. Don't worry, I'll only buy organic food if that will make you happier."

"No. We'll try the Vietnamese restaurant. I'm sure you'll like it and afterwards we'll go to the opera. I queued up all lunch break and managed to get us tickets."

It hadn't taken him long to revert to his normal

pattern of making plans to suit himself and half bullying her into accepting them. Leah didn't intend to return to hiding her disappointment and pretending to be grateful.

"I don't want to do that, Adam. You wanted me to come back with you so we could talk and sort things out. I think that's exactly what we should do."

"All right then. You cook. You might as well choose whatever you like as you've obviously already made your mind up."

Leah decided not to let his lack of enthusiasm put her off and mentally planned her menu to include all his favourite foods. Duncan phoned while she was shopping.

"How are you, Leah?"

"I'm fine. I'm sorry I haven't been in touch."

"It's OK. Jayne explained."

Leah didn't dare ask what the explanation had been. "How are you, Duncan? I've missed you."

She said the last bit without meaning to, but it was the truth.

"Actually, I've had some very good news. My dad has gone into remission. They don't know for how long, but when I visited him last time it seemed we were about to lose him, so this is great news."

"That's wonderful."

"It is. I was wondering... would you like to meet my parents? I'm coming to London tomorrow and well, I sort of mentioned you were in London too and they said they'd love me to bring you to see them."

Leah was torn. She so wanted to see Duncan and meet his parents and hated the idea of disappointing a sick man and his worried wife, but it wasn't fair to Adam to make plans with Duncan just before talking to him and deciding if their relationship could survive.

"I would like to meet them, but it's a bit difficult..."

"Leah, don't sound so worried. I'm sorry if it seemed I was trying to push you into it. It doesn't have to be tomorrow. They're not expecting you, it's just... I couldn't come to London without trying to see you."

"It'd be good to see you again too."

"Hark at us, sounds like we haven't seen each other for weeks."

"It feels like it," she admitted.

"Then meet my parents tomorrow and come back home to Winkleigh Marsh afterwards."

His tone was light and teasing, but she was sure he'd like her to accept.

"Can I call you tomorrow and, um if I..." She didn't know what she meant.

"Of course you can. Maybe I'll get to see you after all?"

"Yes, maybe."

Adam pushed his artichoke around his plate and brushed aside her questions about work.

She tried a different approach. "Shall we give your parents a call? Say you've proposed and I'd like to meet them?"

"I'll ring them tomorrow. It's a bit late now."

"It's seven o'clock."

"I don't usually ring in the evening."

Leah took away their half eaten starters. She put the skewers of king prawns she'd marinated in lime and coconut under the grill and took in the mustard salad and fragrant rice. That gave her time to force a cheerful expression onto her face.

"OK, call tomorrow then. Shall we say we'll go this weekend?"

"They'd need a bit more notice than that."

"I didn't mean we'd stay with them, just call in for a cup of tea or perhaps go out for lunch?"

"We'll see," he said and served himself with rice and prawns.

That was so obviously a no, she decided to change tack again.

"Have you thought where we might live if we married?"

"What's wrong with here?"

"Nothing for a single couple, but there's nowhere

for family to stay and I'd like my parents to be able to visit us and of course, if we had children..."

"Children? Aren't you getting a bit ahead of yourself? You're not even wearing my ring."

He planned his finances years ahead, yet wouldn't discuss the possibility of children with the woman he said he wanted to marry?

"When were you thinking we'd get married?"

He drained his wine glass. "You want to set a date now?"

"Well roughly. We'll need to give our parents plenty of notice, won't we?"

"I suppose so."

"This year?"

"No, I don't think so." He refilled their wine glasses.

"Next year?"

"Maybe."

"Sometime, never?"

"What do you mean?" He pushed his plate away.

"That I don't think anything's changed. You've bought me a ring..."

"Which you're not wearing."

"Which I'm not wearing, so nothing has changed." She too abandoned her food.

"I don't really see why it should have."

"I wasn't happy, Adam."

"Well, no. But that's because of the work, er, problem. We'll sort that out. Actually, I have an idea about that."

"Oh?" He hadn't wanted to discuss it five minutes ago.

"We could re-mortgage the flat and use the money to pay back into Mr Gilmore-Bunce's account. I think I've found a way to do that without it being traced, but you can see why buying a bigger home would be difficult right now."

"Adam, are you crazy? I didn't steal that money. Why on earth should I pay it back?"

"It would clear your name and get your job back. In the long run, I think we'd be better off."

"No we wouldn't. The investigation will clear my name. I'm not at all sure I want my job back, but even if I did, I don't think they'll suddenly start trusting me just because the money mysteriously reappeared."

They didn't speak as they played with their raspberry tart and crème fraîche, finished the wine and drank their coffee.

He helped her stack the dishwasher, but they were so awkwardly careful not to touch each other that the process would have been much easier if she'd done it on her own.

"I'm going for a walk," she said.

"Shall I come with you?"

"No, I want to think. I'll take my phone and stay nearby. I'll be fine."

Leah thought of ringing Jayne, but she didn't need to. She knew her advice would be to, 'Leave him and come back here.'

She was tempted to ring Duncan too and hoped he'd say much the same thing. She was almost sure he would, but she couldn't find out, still less agree until she'd finished things with Adam. It was what she had to do. She didn't want to marry him and she didn't want to stay in London. Nothing she missed about the city couldn't be met by a day's sight seeing or occasional trip to the theatre. Everything Leah wanted was in Winkleigh Marsh and that included Duncan.

Leah let herself back into the flat, collected the ring box by the side of the bed and handed it to Adam.

"I'm so sorry, I can't marry you. I want to go back to Primrose Cottage and live there."

For what seemed like a long time Adam didn't speak or react at all. Then he took a deep breath, swallowed several times and asked, "You'll take the job you were offered?"

She nodded. She wasn't sure if she would, but that was a possibility and something Adam might understand.

"I can't stop you, but I think you're making a mistake. You've had a couple of months holiday there and it's reminded you of your childhood, but that's not real life, Leah."

"To me it is."

"I think you'll change your mind. If you do, well you know where I am."

"Thank you." She hugged him in gratitude. She hadn't hoped he'd be so accepting or so nice. Maybe she should have felt hurt he'd taken the news so well, but she just felt relieved.

"How about the opera? I still have the tickets."

"Lovely."

It wasn't lovely; Adam seemed in shock and she felt guilty for hurting him, but it was a lot better than spending the evening in the flat with a man she'd just dumped.

Leah had arranged to meet Duncan outside the flat as it didn't seem right to invite him to Adam's home. She shoved her cases onto the back seat and jumped into the car beside him. He pulled her into a hug.

"You OK?" he asked.

She was. Once she was in Duncan's arms, her last few doubts and worries seemed to melt away. "Yes. I've told Adam it's over and he's taken it very well."

"Never mind him. Are you OK?"

She tilted her head up until her lips brushed against his. Duncan returned her kiss.

A car beeped its horn and he released her.

"I'm more than OK. The driver behind isn't though, you'd better get going."

"Leah, I have a confession to make," Duncan told her as he drove away.

"Oh?"

"My parents sort of got the idea we're thinking of getting married and I didn't correct them."

"Why not?"

"Because in my case it's true and because it's what Dad wants to believe. He's worried about carrying on the family name and stuff."

He was thinking of marrying her? She wanted to jump up and down or dance, but there wasn't room in the car. She wanted to kiss him but it wasn't safe as he was driving. She wanted to ask him to explain. Have him say it again but there wasn't the time. They'd arrived at the nursing home.

If Leah hadn't known where they were going, she'd have assumed he'd taken her to a fancy hotel that just happened to have a lot of medical staff wandering about. Duncan led her to the suite his parents were sharing.

Duncan kissed his mother, hugged his dad and introduced Leah.

"We're so pleased to meet you, my dear," his mum

246

said. "Would you like some tea? Here let me take your coat."

"Stop fussing, woman," his dad said. "Come here, Leah and let me get a proper look at you."

Obediently she went over to him.

"You really are as pretty as he said you were. I know it's not official yet, but welcome to the family."

"Thank you, Mr er..."

"Call me Dad, might as well start as we mean to go on."

"Yes." She was glad Duncan had warned her, even if that hadn't fully prepared her for the reception she was getting.

"Now, promise me you won't take too long setting a date. I'm quite well enough to attend a wedding now and I want something to look forward to."

Leah glanced about for support. Duncan looked as though he was trying not to laugh, but his mum came to her rescue.

"Leave her be, you're embarrassing the poor girl."

"What's to be embarrassed about? Getting married's perfectly natural. Didn't say she was to hurry up and give us grandchildren, did I?"

"Men!" His mum turned to Leah. "I'd like to tell you my dear son only takes after me, but I'm afraid that wouldn't be strictly true."

"Good job too. Wouldn't get anywhere if we were

to hang around waiting for you women to make up your minds, would we, my boy?"

"No Dad, we wouldn't. But let me make my own proposal, eh?"

"All right, but do it soon."

"Yes, Dad."

Fortunately a trolley laden with tea and cakes was brought in at that moment. After that, the conversation became more normal

"Sorry about Dad," Duncan said as they left the nursing home and headed back for Winkleigh Marsh.

"Don't be, I liked him. Both of them."

"Good .They liked you too. If they don't like people they're just very, very polite. It's really quite scary."

"They didn't scare me."

"And what about the things Dad was suggesting?"

"That didn't scare me either."

"No?"

"I'm not agreeing to anything, but if you were to ask me properly sometime then I probably wouldn't scream and run away."

Chapter 14

Jayne had to wait to greet Leah as Tarragon got there first. She gave her a hug, then said, "Well, get changed, you can't clean out the pigs in that lot."

Leah gave a mock salute, collected her case and strode towards Primrose Cottage. Duncan picked up her remaining bags, but Jayne grabbed his arm to stop him following. Leah didn't have long to speculate about what Jayne was telling him as he soon caught her up.

"Fancy going out for a drink tonight?"

"I do, but not for too long. I rather suspect Jayne's going to want to interrogate me and it's been quite an emotional couple of days."

He hugged her close. "Of course. I'm just being selfish. You talk to Jayne and sort yourself out and I'll leave off pestering you until tomorrow. I promise not to come calling before it's light."

"I do like you an awful lot," she told him.

"I'm rather counting on that." He kissed her in a way that proved he liked her an awful lot too.

Leah got changed and found Jayne at the pigsty.

"Aaaw, they're adorable!"

"They are. I've already started wondering if I should keep one to breed from."

"Definitely!"

"Maybe. Depends if I'll have any help cleaning them out."

"You will."

As the two women fed the orphan lambs and gave all the animals fresh bedding, Leah started briefing Jayne on all that had happened since Adam took her away from Winkleigh Marsh.

"He took it OK, you dumping him?"

"Yes, I'd worried he might get nasty, but he was fine. He brought me a coffee before he went to work this morning and said there was no rush for me to move all my stuff out. He hopes I'll change my mind, but if not then he's going to sell the flat as there would be too many memories."

"Trying to make you feel guilty?"

"No, I don't think so. He thinks me coming down here is just a fad and I'll be back as soon as I can go back to work."

"What about Jim's offer?"

"I'll go in and see what's involved, but I can't start working there until my name has been cleared and I've officially left Prophet Margin."

"Now to the important bit. What about Duncan?"

"You'll have to ply me with cowslip wine to get

me to talk."

Jayne did just that after their supper. Leah admitted she wanted to spend the rest of her life living on a farm with Duncan.

"I'm pretty sure that's what he wants too," Jayne said. She refilled their glasses.

"Yes and his parents."

"You've met them? Then you know..."

"About his dad?"

"Yes."

"He was fine when I saw him. In remission they said and there's a good chance he'll stay like that for quite a while." Leah told Jayne about the visit and everything Duncan's dad had said.

The warmth of the fire and the effects of the wine soon had both women yawning and they agreed an early night would be a good idea.

"Leah, wake up!" Jayne shook her.

She must be dreaming. She hadn't set her alarm, but even if she'd slept late, Jayne wouldn't be yelling at her.

"Leah, you've got to get up! Come on!" Jayne dragged the quilt off Leah and pulled at her arm.

"Milk your own cow."

"There's a fire, get up!"

Leah pulled on clothes at random and raced down

the stairs after Jayne.

The barn was blazing and the cows were bellowing in fear. She could hear the dog barking and the lambs and pigs were all making a horrible racket.

"Where's Tarragon?"

"I shut him in the pick-up. He was hysterical and would have panicked the other animals. Let's get the cows first, we can put them in a field, they'll be OK."

They let the terrified cattle out just in time. The heat was intense and burning straw was falling dangerously close to their bedding.

"What next?"

"We need pens or something to put the rest in. God Leah, we can't let them burn."

"We won't, we won't. How about gates? Could we make a pen from them for the lambs?"

"Yes, that would work."

They dragged gates from their hinges and carried them a safe distance from the flames. Once they were lashed together, they carried the lambs two at a time into the pen.

"The chickens will be OK, the flames are going the other way, but I'm worried about the piglets. I just don't see how we can make them a pen in time."

"Shall we just let them out? They might get hurt if they just run away, but thier chances would be better than if they're caught in the fire."

"All right, I suppose so."

They ran to the pigsty. The wall was already hot.

"The chicken run, that would hold them," Jayne said. "It's not ideal, but we'll try that."

"OK. Jayne, did you call the fire brigade?"

Jayne sagged as though she'd been hit. "No."

"I'll do it." Leah, wishing she hadn't lost her habit of carrying her mobile at all times, turned and ran toward the house.

"No." Jayne pulled her arm. "Look."

Leah looked where Jayne pointed. A burning telegraph pole crashed down towards the cottage, blocking her route.

"You're not going in there," Jayne said.

"We need help."

"Take the pick-up. I'll move the pigs."

Leah drove as fast as she dared over the fields to Home Farm. In her panic, she'd forgotten the dog. Poor Tarragon cowered on the floor in front of the passenger seat. He knew there was something terribly wrong and must think his banishment to the pick-up meant he was getting the blame.

"It's OK, boy," she tried to reassure him. That didn't seem to help, but when she added, "I'm glad you're with me," he thumped his tail. That was probably because what she said that time was true and it made her voice sound more reassuring.

Twice Leah stopped to open gates which she didn't close. Once she crashed through a post and rail fence. She doubted even G-B would put the inconvenience of cows in the wrong field and broken timber above the safety of Jayne's animals and Primrose Cottage.

She blasted the horn as she drove into the yard, then hammered on Mr Gilmore-Bunce's door. Tarragon accompanied her, sticking closer than if he'd been on a lead. Leah tried to call out that there was a fire, but first her voice, then her legs failed her. She slumped against the door frame.

"Leah?" It was Duncan, wearing just jeans and pulling on a shirt.

"Duncan, thank God!"

"Leah, what is it?" He pulled her into his arms and stroked her matted, smoky hair.

She wanted to stay in his arms and let him comfort her, but there wasn't time.

"Jayne's barn's on fire and we can't get in the house to call for help."

"Go in, the phone is first on the left. Call the fire brigade, then come out into the yard. Better leave Tarragon here."

Duncan had the pick-up turned round when she came out. She jumped in next to him. He drove back at even greater speed than Leah had used to get there.

"I've grabbed the pump from the inspection pit, so we'll be able to do something before the fire brigade

254

get there. Here, take my phone and call Phil for me."

Leah searched his contacts for a Phil and held the phone for Duncan to speak.

"There's a fire at Primrose Cottage. Meet me there, but first call Jake and get him to stand by the main road and direct the fire brigade down the lane."

Duncan followed the tracks Leah had made in the damp ground, making no comments about the damage and open gates.

At Jayne's cottage Duncan got the women to lug a hose to the stream while he connected his pump to a generator he'd brought. They hosed down the side of Primrose Cottage.

The fire brigade soon arrived, followed promptly by Phil and Jake. Those two men helped Duncan and the women make a better pen for the lambs and provide them with a little salvaged bedding. They also put a sprinkling of straw down for the piglets and carted in a water trough.

By the time they'd finished, the fire brigade had the blaze under control.

An officer said, "We'll stay 'til we're sure there's no chance of it re-igniting. Your house seems fine, but I don't want you going back in there tonight. Is there anyone you can go to?"

"Yes," Duncan said. "They'll come to Home Farm."

"Good, we'll be back in the morning to do an

assessment, but I expect you'll be able to return then."

Duncan guided the shocked women to the pick-up. "I'll just give the fire brigade our contact details."

He drove them, and the dog, at a sensible speed back to Home Farm. Exhausted, Leah and Jayne collapsed into the double bed Duncan offered them.

Leah awoke in a strange bed, aware of someone next to her and the smell of smoke. She couldn't move her legs, but she could hear a woman crying; Jayne. That meant the events of last night weren't just an awful dream.

"Shh, shh. We got all the animals out," Leah said, hugging Jayne.

The weight on Leah's legs moved as Tarragon scrambled up to lick his mistress's face.

"Did we? I don't remember. I panicked."

"Yes, but while you were panicking, you were saving them. All of them."

"Leah? Jayne?" Duncan whispered through the door.

"We're awake," Leah replied.

He came in, carrying an armful of clothes. "These are Mum's, she'd want you to have them. I've made some tea, I'll bring that up, then leave you in peace."

Duncan returned with a tray loaded with tea, toast

and biscuits. "Bathroom is just next door. Please help yourself to anything you want."

"Thanks," Jayne whispered.

"Yes, thank you, Duncan." Leah wanted to know why he had been sleeping at Oliver Gilmore-Bunce's house, but couldn't bring herself to say anything. She'd jumped to enough conclusions about G-B already.

After a shower and breakfast, the women both felt much better, even in their borrowed clothes.

"Jayne, doesn't it seem odd to you that Duncan was sleeping here last night?"

"No. Where would you expect him to sleep?"

"I, well..." She'd imagined herself sleeping with him, but never considered where that might be. "He lives in? OK that makes sense, but surely his mother can't live here too?" She indicated the clothes Duncan had given them.

"I thought you... You'd best ask him, I think."

"I will."

She didn't get the chance for quite some time. Jayne and Duncan discussed plans for getting food and bedding for her animals as he drove them back to Primrose Cottage. When they got there, Jim had arrived. He hugged Jayne, then Leah.

Poor man looked as though he'd been crying. He told them he'd heard about the fire and drove straight over. "There was no one here and you didn't answer your phone."

"Oh, Jim. I'm so sorry you were worried. We're fine, look."

Jim stared at Jayne then glanced at Leah before nodding his head.

"The animals too. Everyone's safe," Jayne assured him.

Together, the four of them heard the fire officer's assessment. They learned the barn and the cattle and sheep pens were unsafe and would have to be demolished after a further investigation was carried out to find the cause of the fire. All the hay and straw was ruined, plus a lot of equipment and the thatch on the cottage needed replacing.

"It did anyway," Jayne told him. "It's safe to go in though, is it?"

"Yes, the damage to the house is just superficial."

They thanked him.

"And thank you, Duncan," Jayne said. "I'm going to see if I can salvage anything to feed the lambs with. Your men dragged out a lot of stuff from the barn so I think I'll be lucky. Duncan, Leah wants to know why you're living at Home Farm."

"Ah. Yes."

Jayne called Tarragon, grabbed Jim's hand and left them.

"I expect there's a simple explanation?" Leah asked hopefully. Almost any explanation would have satisfied her as long as it meant she could fall into his arms and have him hold her tight for a long time.

"There is. I'm Oliver Gilmore-Bunce."

"Who? What?"

"Oliver Duncan Alan Gilmore-Bunce, to be precise."

"You can't be."

"Yes I can. I'm named after my dad, Oliver Thomas Cyril Gilmore-Bunce. All the men in the family have been called Oliver, so we use one of our middle names. Home Farm is my home, I took over the business when Dad got ill."

"You are Oliver Gilmore-Bunce?" He couldn't be. Leah could feel her body shaking and her nails digging painfully into her palms, but she couldn't do anything to stop it. All those things she'd said about him. How could he have made such a fool of her?

"I thought you cared about me, perhaps even loved me and that we had a future together and instead you've been lying to me the whole time."

"Lying? About what?"

"Your name. You said you were Duncan. Everyone said you were Duncan."

"And so I am. I usually only give my full name on tax returns, but if I'd realised I'd ever be accused of misleading you, I'd have given the full ten syllable version while you sank deeper into the mud." He sounded as angry as she felt.

259

He had a point, but he must have known she'd thought he and G-B were two separate people. Of course he did, he'd let her rant about the awful things G-B had done and never once even tried to tell her the truth. He was as manipulative and deceitful as she'd always thought him.

"You said... you let me think... Adam wanted to marry me and I said no because I thought... " Her sobs prevented her saying more. She couldn't think of anything except that Duncan had lied and because of that she'd told him she hated him. That made her a bigger liar than he was.

"I do care, Leah. I love you, I want to marry you and..." He tried to put his arms around her, but she pushed him away.

"Don't touch me."

"Leah please."

"If you love someone you don't lie to them."

"I didn't, I just..."

"Go, just go." She pushed past him and ran for the safety of Primrose Cottage.

He'd have to walk home, but she didn't care. She slammed the door, sank against it and sobbed. Eventually she heard her phone ringing. She scrambled to find it and flipped it open. It was Rachel calling. Another sob escaped her. She'd hoped it would be Duncan and he'd somehow found something to say that would make everything all right.

The phone kept ringing, so she answered.

It was Rachel. "Leah, I've got great news. Adam Ferrand has been arrested!"

Chapter 15

"In what way can that possibly be good news?" Leah demanded.

"He's the one who stole the client's money. You're in the clear, Leah. You can come back to Prophet Margin anytime you want."

"Adam stole the money and framed me?"

"Well, it's not quite as simple as that. He didn't actually steal anything. Well technically I suppose he did, but not for himself. He made some bad investments for his clients, then tried to cover it up by moving money around. Apparently, he kept hoping to make enough to replace what he'd moved and cover his tracks and it would probably have worked if Mr Gilmore-Bunce hadn't needed the money for his father's medical care."

Poor Duncan, already worried about his father, he'd discovered the company he'd trusted with his money had defrauded him.

Rachel continued, "Adam said he hadn't meant to implicate you, but he'd needed to use another account and had got lucky and guessed your passwords. He knew you were completely honest, so didn't think anyone would ever seriously consider you guilty. I think he was telling the truth. He seemed genuinely upset about the problems he'd caused you and worried about what you'd think."

She was glad now their relationship had been kept secret or she might have been implicated in the fraud. Not that it really mattered, she realised. As she had no intention of returning to Prophet Margin it didn't matter what they thought. What about Duncan though? What was his opinion of her, would the latest news change that and did she care anyway?

"Are you OK?" Rachel asked.

"Not really. This is a bit of a shock."

"Yes, it must be."

"Thanks for letting me know, Rachel and for all you've done."

"No problem. You'll be getting all this officially in a day or so. Just thought you'd like to know as soon as possible."

They agreed to talk then, after Leah had a chance to think about the news. She couldn't think though, not about anything positive. Everything she'd wanted was lost to her. She couldn't even cry, just sat on the floor staring into space and feeling numb.

After a while she felt something wet on her hand. It was Tarragon gently nudging her.

"Good boy, you never lie to me, do you?" She wrapped her body around his. The dog lay placid as though sharing her pain.

"Leah?" Jayne said from the doorway. "Can I come in?"

"Of course."

Jayne came closer.

"What am I going to do?" Leah sobbed.

"About what, lovey?" She lowered herself onto the floor next to Leah and took her hand.

"Everything. It's all gone wrong. I wanted Duncan but now I hate him and he hates me. I thought I wanted to marry Adam, but when he proposed I didn't want to anymore and... Oh you don't know. It was him, he stole the money. Sort of."

"Adam? And blamed you? That ba... But he did care about you, I saw that. How could he do it?"

"I don't know. It's complicated. He made a mistake and then I suppose he just got caught up in things. He never could admit if he was wrong."

"So, do they think you were involved?"

Leah shook her head. "I could go back to Prophet Margin, if I wanted to but I don't. But that doesn't matter. Your farm, Jayne. I wanted to stay here, but it's worse for you. This is your life and it's gone up in smoke."

"No love, not my life, just a barn. I'm insured. I'll get another barn built. I haven't lost anything important. I'll carry on and you're more than welcome to stay. There's plenty of work to be done."

"Thanks, Jayne." Leah hugged her. "At least I can

rely on you."

"Now what's all this nonsense about hating Duncan?"

"He lied to me."

"No. There was a bit of confusion over his name. It's not like he was committing fraud."

"No, it's worse. Adam was just trying to cover up his mistake. Duncan lied about who he really is. He knew how I felt about him and he deliberately tricked me into saying horrible things about him."

"Rubbish! When did he lie?"

"All the time. Right from the start."

"No, that was me. I knew who he was, but you were so against Oliver Gilmore-Bunce I didn't think you'd give him a chance, so I didn't tell you who he was. Duncan wanted to be honest with you, but I convinced him to wait."

"You lied? Yes, I suppose you did, but... Oh I don't know about anything anymore."

"The sheep need feeding. Nothing like a bit of work to clear your head." Jayne stood up, then hauled Leah to her feet. "What on earth's happened to your boots?"

Leah looked down at her feet. "I stomped out some burning straw last night, must have melted them a bit."

"A bit? Aren't they uncomfortable?"

"Not really, but I guess they'll leak."

"Better wear the spare ones again."

Jayne was right, being out in the sunshine and doing something constructive did make her feel better. Her life wasn't over. She had a home with Jayne and the offer of a job with Jim. Things were better than when she'd driven down to Winkleigh Marsh earlier in the year, even if it didn't feel as though they were.

Leah grabbed a bale of hay and carried it into the sheep field. Remembering how she'd been unable to lift one on her own when she came made her realise how much she'd changed physically. She didn't seem to have developed much emotionally though as her irrational dislike of G-B still seemed to be clouding her judgement. Was she going to believe Adam's opinion of the man, or that of Jayne and her own heart?

She stomped across to where the sheep were usually fed, only then noticing that the metal rack had been moved from its previous position. Jayne must have done that while Leah was in London. She wondered why as she changed course and walked towards it.

The answer came to her just too late. Where the sheep had repeatedly gathered in the same spot they'd churned up the ground, turning it to deep, heavy mud. Leah, weighed down with the bale, was stuck just as she had been before. This time her phone wasn't flat; it was in Primrose Cottage. She didn't even have Tarragon with her.

"Want some help?"

She couldn't turn to see who had asked but she didn't need to. Duncan's deep voice was unmistakable.

"I can get myself out," she snapped. Immediately she felt guilty. She was as angry with herself as she was with him.

"Really?"

Not without leaving the boots behind, she couldn't.

"You weren't carrying a bale of hay last time. At least let me take that."

She didn't protest as he came closer and took the heavy bale from her aching hands. He took it to the hay rack and put it in place, removed the strings so the sheep could eat the hay, then returned slowly to stand before her.

If only she could turn back time to when they'd first met and start again without the lies.

"Can't we start again?" he asked.

She didn't answer. Just because they wanted the same thing didn't mean it was possible.

"Hi. I'm Oliver Duncan Alan Gilmore-Bunce. Please call me Duncan, nearly everyone does. By the way, I haven't accused you of fraud, I just asked Prophet Margin why there wasn't as much money in my account as I'd expected and they promised to

267

investigate. Sorry about the abrupt instructions I sent regarding my family's investments, but I'd just taken over that side of things, it didn't really interest me and I was worried about Dad."

She hung her head. Of course he couldn't have explained all that at their first meeting, particularly as he had no idea where she worked or that she'd care what name was on his birth certificate.

"Hi, I'm Leah-May Jayne Tilbury," she mumbled. "I used to live with the man who embezzled your savings. I believed the lies he told me about you rather than the evidence of your actions and the assurances of Jayne. I'm a complete idiot who can't even walk across a field without getting stuck."

He raised an eyebrow and smiled slightly. "OK if I call you Leah?"

She gave a small nod.

"I want to rescue you, Leah. That's all I've wanted since I first saw you."

It's all she'd wanted then and all she wanted now. She looked up at him and tried to smile.

Duncan strode over and lifted her free of the mud. He pulled her close and wrapped his arms around her, leaving her bare feet dangling well above ground level.

"I love you," he said.

She clung on to him as he kissed her passionately.

"You've left my wellies behind," she giggled.

"Good. I don't want you running away from me."

"I won't, never again." She wrapped her legs around his hips and held on tight.

"Oh dear," he said as he strode back with her towards the farmyard.

"What?"

"Just when I really need a hay barn, it's been burned down."

Her heart beat faster and she was glad she was already off her feet as she doubted her legs would hold her. "There's one at Home Farm," she suggested hopefully.

"There is. Do you think Aunt Jayne will lend me her pick-up?"

"Yes, but not if you call her Aunt Jayne."

"She'll have to get used to it when we're married and she's part of the family."

"You haven't proposed yet," she pointed out.

"But I will." He sat her in the pick-up and went in search of Jayne.

As he drove her back to Home Farm, still with only socks on her feet, Leah remembered her relief when he'd opened the door to her the night before. She remembered too that he'd been hastily pulling on his clothes. At the time, she'd been far too worried to appreciate the sight of him half naked. Things were different now. Leah reached out a hand towards the button on his nearest shirt sleeve and tried to undo it.

269

"Patience woman," he said.

He didn't stop to close gates as he drove through, so she guessed he was in almost as much of a hurry as she was. Duncan abandoned the pick-up outside the house and carried Leah up the path. It seemed picky to point out the barn was in totally the other direction. She took the keys from his pocket and unlocked the door to let them in. She was already tugging his shirt up when he released his grip, allowing her feet to touch the floor. His shirt came off over his head as he kicked the door shut behind them and pulled Leah into his arms.

I hope you enjoyed Escape To The Country. If you did, I'd very much appreciate you leaving a review on Amazon, Goodreads or anywhere else.

To learn more about my writing life, hear about new releases and get a free short ebook, news and competitions, sign up to my newsletter – subscribepage.io/ItLSNa or you can find the link on my website patsycollins.uk

More books by Patsy Collins

Novels –

Leave Nothing But Footprints

Firestarter

Paint Me A Picture

A Year And A Day

Acting Like A Killer

Little Mallow cosy mystery series

Disguised Murder and Community Spirit in Little
Mallow
Dependable Friends and Deceitful Neighbours in
Little Mallow

Short story collections –

Over The Garden Fence
Up The Garden Path
Through The Garden Gate
In The Garden Air
Beyond The Garden Gate

No Family Secrets
Can't Choose Your Family
Family Feeling
Keep It In The Family
Happy Families

All That Love Stuff
Lots Of Love
With Love And Kisses
Love Is The Answer

Slightly Spooky Stories I
Slightly Spooky Stories II
Slightly Spooky Stories III
Slightly Spooky Stories IV
Slightly Spooky Stories V

Perfect Timing
Just A Job
Coffee & Cake

A Way With Words
Dressed To Impress
Criminal Intent
Crime In Mind
Making A Move
Days To Remember
A Clean Bill Of Health

Non-fiction –

Form Story Idea to Reader -
An accessible guide to writing fiction co-authored
with Rosemary J. Kind

A Year Of Ideas: 365 sets of writing prompts and
exercises

Printed in Great Britain
by Amazon

46756510R00155